The one packing Longarm's side arm and, doubtless, a lot of his other belongings, swung to face the man he'd robbed. Longarm strode closer to that one to say, "I was only sent to bring in Harmony Drake. Would you rather fight another man's fight or make a deal?"

The kid wearing Longarm's gun blustered, "You ain't got any jurisdiction down this way and, come to study on it, I could give a little whistle and have you gunned down like a dog by those *rurales*."

The one in the far corner, who must have thought Longarm didn't know they were together, suddenly tipped his thick oak table forward and dropped behind it to make mysterious movements of his own. Longarm swung the muzzle of the Big Fifty up to fire a shot heard all across Puerto Peñasco . . .

TABOR EVANS

LONGARM

AND THE
BIG FIFTY

J

JOVE BOOKS, NEW YORK

LONGARM AND THE BIG FIFTY

A Jove Book / published by arrangement with
the author

PRINTING HISTORY
Jove edition / July 1996

All rights reserved.
Copyright © 1996 by Jove Publications, Inc.
This book may not be reproduced in whole
or in part, by mimeograph or any other means,
without permission. For information address:
The Berkley Publishing Group, 200 Madison Avenue,
New York, New York 10016.

The Putnam Berkley World Wide Web site address is
http://www.berkley.com

ISBN: 0-515-11895-8

A JOVE BOOK®
Jove Books are published by The Berkley Publishing Group,
200 Madison Avenue, New York, New York 10016.
JOVE and the "J" design are trademarks
belonging to Jove Publications, Inc.

PRINTED IN THE UNITED STATES OF AMERICA

10 9 8 7 6 5 4 3 2 1

Chapter 1

The long, hot summer day had ended, and so Yuma was getting out of bed as Deputy U.S. Marshal Custis Long was finishing his supper in a stand-up *cafetin* across the plaza from the jailhouse. The fish pie was tempting, but he had chores to do and and a train to catch. So Longarm, as he was better known to friend and foe alike, washed down the last of his hot tamales with tepid black coffee and settled up with the pretty Mexican counter gal, leaving her a dime tip to show he hadn't ignored her batty eyelashes because he'd thought she was too fat. Then he paused by the newsstand out front to light a three-for-a-nickel cheroot and grimace down at the evening headlines.

As if folks along the lower Gila didn't have enough to worry them, the fool *Arizona Advocate* was blaring, "APACHE OUT ON WARPATH!"

You couldn't buy the *Tombstone Epitaph* around the central plaza. So there was no sweet voice of reason from old John Clum, the former BIA agent who'd given up educating Indians to publish his own newspaper for cowboys and such to read. The last edition of the *Epitaph* read by Longarm had explained how unlikely it would be for Victorio and his reservation-jumpers to raid west of, say, Apache

Pass in high summer. It was scandalous to scare folks like that just to sell a few more copies of your otherwise dull newspaper.

President Hayes and his first lady, Miss Lemonade Lucy, had made it clear they expected all federal employees, including lawmen, to dress and behave like ribbon clerks or bank tellers. But since neither of them came out to Arizona Territory in August all that often, Longarm had packed his tweed frock coat and vest away with his infernal tie, and pinned his federal badge to the front of his hickory shirt lest anyone take him for a saddle tramp packing a .44-40 cross-draw.

It was still hotter than the hinges of Hell as he trudged across the dusty plaza. But somewhere in the night a guitar was commencing a lively hat dance and a young gal was standing on a trestle table to light a string of paper lanterns. Longarm didn't ask or even wonder if they were fixing to have a fiesta or just a market night. Once the sun went down in Arizona, everyone felt overdue for *some* damned sort of a celebration.

Longarm had already done the paperwork at the jailhouse when he'd arrived that morning aboard the westbound Southern Pacific, so they had Harmony Drake out front and ready to go. Or out front in cuffs and leg irons, whether he wanted to go or not.

One of the Arizona lawmen who'd been holding the killer on a federal warrant for Longarm to pick up confided cheerfully that the prisoner seemed mighty sad for a sport who killed other folks with such a carefree attitude. "Old Harmony turnt down both his dinner and a finer supper than he deserved," the lawman said. "Says he's feeling poorly. Reckon they told him how you crap your pants when they hang you and he's hoping to hold down the stink."

Longarm had never cottoned to gallows humor aimed at victims in no position to enjoy it. So he simply nodded at the seated prisoner, perhaps a tad younger and too overdressed for the occasion, and said, "We'll be leaving now, Mister Drake. I got us a coach seat aboard the night train to Deming. I'm sorry you have to wear those leg irons. But they're what you get for escaping the last time anyone tried to transport you cross-country. We'll be seated by a window and you may need that denim jacket as this desert air cools off after dark. But right now you're sweating like a pig, and I reckon we'd best get you down to shirtsleeves before we leave."

Earlier, Longarm had given the Arizona jailors the cuffs and leg irons the prisoner was wearing. So he fumbled the little key from the fob pocket of his tweed pants to unlock the cuffs as Harmony Drake's rusty-sounding voice creaked, "I ain't sweating because I feel hot. I feel like I'm coming *down* with something. Something serious as hell."

Longarm helped the uncuffed prisoner out of his sweat-soaked though thin denim jacket as he calmly replied, "We have to lay over betwixt trains at Deming, just across the New Mexico line. If the cool night ride ain't cheered you up, I'll have a sawbones look you over before we head on up to Colorado."

Drake said he doubted he'd last that long. The local lawman who'd made rude remarks about his date with the hangman suggested he die on his way there and save everyone a heap of trouble.

Longarm snapped the cuffs back in place and draped the limp denim jacket over the shining steel links as he helped the condemned killer to stand up, quietly saying, "The train depot ain't but a furlong or so to walk. Do you reckon you can make it without help?"

Harmony Drake said, "Not hardly," and sat back down, adding it felt as if someone had drained all the juice out of his legs and that he had a bellyache as well.

Another local jailer snorted, "He's goldbricking you, Longarm. He ain't sick. He just don't want you to carry him back to that Colorado court's jurisdiction."

The thought had already occurred to Longarm. But even a convicted killer had been known to take sick like other mortals. So he got out his pocket watch, cussed it, and decided, "I could use some help from you gents in bearing him from here to that railroad platform."

He could see nobody seemed anxious to leap at such an opportunity. So he fished out some smokes to distribute as he quietly added, "If he dies aboard the train, it'll be all my misfortune and none of your own."

So after they'd all lit up, they improvised a litter to carry the moaning and groaning Harmony Drake down the way, and cheerfully helped Longarm get him aboard the 8:15 eastbound.

In the time they had left while the engine took on water for the first leg of its desert run, Longarm cuffed his prisoner's right-hand wrist to the arm of his seat against the south-facing window and gave him a cheroot and some waterproof Mexican matches, murmuring, "I have to ask the conductor something. Don't go 'way, unless you want a bullet where it might smart, and I'll be back directly."

Harmony Drake said he didn't feel like smoking. He asked if Longarm would mind removing his leg irons seeing he was secured to the seat and it felt better when he held his right knee up as high as he could get it.

Longarm had hoped the rascal wouldn't say anything like that. He muttered, "When I come back. I know what you're trying to sell me. I ain't sure I'm ready to buy it. But just sit tight and like the old hymn goes, farther along we'll know more about it."

Then he strode up the aisle and into the car beyond, where sure enough, he caught the grizzled conductor flirting with a gal young enough to be his granddaughter.

Ticking the brim of his Stetson to the gal, Longarm curtly cut in to ask the older man if they'd be stopping to jerk water at the Gila Bend Indian Agency.

The conductor nodded and said, "East- or westbound,

4

we always jerk water at Gila Bend. Why do you ask, Deputy?''

Longarm explained, "I'm carrying a prisoner back to Colorado with a bellyache. Leastways, he says he's got a bellyache, with a fever. I thought I'd like to have the sawbones at that Indian agency take a look and tell me I'm just acting like an old fuss."

The gal chimed in to say with a smile that she was not connected in any way with the Bureau of Indian Affairs, but that she worked as a nurse out of the Deming Dispensary if he was in the market for her modest medical opinions.

He declared he surely was. So all three of them went on back to find Harmony Drake writhing on the floor between the seats like a sick wolverine with one paw caught in a trap.

The gal, whose light hair and coloring went by the name of Sister Ilsa Anders, stamped a foot and told him to behave like a big brave boy if he expected her to give him a proper medical examination.

Harmony Drake stared goggle-eyed, laughed more like a silly kid than a big brave boy, and asked if she cared to give him an *improper* going-over.

Longarm told him to behave, and got him back up on the seat as the train was pulling out of the depot with a mournful tolling of its engine bell. When Ilsa asked him to free the prisoner's ankles, Longarm did so, and sure enough, Drake hauled his right knee up to hug against his belly with his free arm, gasping, "Oh, Lord, that feels much better!"

The ash-blonde perched on her knees in the empty seat in front to reach over and feel Drake's forehead with the back of her hand, sadly wishing aloud for the medical kit she hadn't packed while going to visit her kin in Yuma.

She asked Drake whether he'd been having any chills as well as hot, sweaty spells. When he allowed he had, she made him stick out his tongue. Then she turned to tell Longarm, "It's hard to be sure with not even a proper ther-

5

mometer to work with. It could be nothing more than mesenteric adenitis, albeit he seems a tad old for such childish infections. It could be pyelonephritis of the right kidney, of course.''

Longarm stared morosely out at the window lights of the town they were rapidly leaving as he quietly asked, "Or couldn't it be a mortified appendix, such as Brother Brigham Young just suffered up to Salt Lake City, ma'am?''

The conductor whistled, and allowed he could still stop the train if they wanted to get off.

Longarm was tempted. But then the gal who seemed to know more about such grim matters said, "There are a dozen less dangerous conditions that ape the same symptoms, and he'll do better, no matter what ails him, if you get him to a doctor at a higher and cooler altitude. The muggy heat down at this end of the valley is enough to make anyone with any condition break out in a sweat, and even if this is what I'm sure we all hope it isn't, cooling that abdomen as much as possible is indicated.''

The conductor said they had some ice up in the dining car.

Longarm asked him to go fetch some as he told his prisoner and the volunteer nurse, "We'll put an ice pack aboard and see whether it's better or worse by the time we reach Gila Bend. Unless it's way better, we'd best get off there and stick you in that agency clinic, old son.''

Harmony Drake protested, "I don't want to have that bellyache Brigham Young come down with and died, durn it! Can't you cure me better than them Mormon medicos, ma'am?''

Sister Anders said soothingly, "It may not be anything half as serious as appendicitis, sir. Didn't you just hear me saying there were a lot of other conditions with similar symptoms?''

Harmony Drake insisted, "My gut hurts like fire and you ain't said you can make it better, pretty lady!''

The blonde regarded him with ill-concealed distaste as she told him he'd have more to worry about if the pain suddenly vanished for no apparent reason. The conductor came back with a colored dining car attendant who was packing some linen napkins and a bucket of crushed ice.

The conductor volunteered, "We have a vacant sleeping compartment up forward if you want to operate on him, Sister Anders."

The young blonde sighed and replied, "If only I or anyone else had the skills, or the nerve. Surgeons *have* removed inflamed appendixes, in a hospital, under general anesthesia, and some few of their patients have survived. But the currently accepted procedure calls for bed rest with ice packs and quinine or other febrifuges that may get the patient's temperature down before the inflamed appendix bursts!"

Harmony Drake sobbed that he didn't want his durned appendix busting inside him. Longarm told him not to blubber up, and suggested they get to that compartment, strip him down, and ice his guts good.

The three grown men managed to move him forward three damned cars and change, with the gal fussing at them not to make any sudden moves, as other passengers gaped at them all along the way.

Then they had the condemned killer stretched out atop a bed quilt with his shirt open and his pants half down, despite his protestations that he didn't know Sister Anders that well.

She told him to just hesh as she placed the ice pack in place. It was soggy as hell as the warm night air got right to work on that ice. But Harmony Drake blessed her as an angel of mercy who made Florence Nightingale look like a witch on a broom, and allowed that he was feeling a whole lot better already.

The blonde's worried blue eyes met Longarm's. She indicated by a slight motion of her head that there were some

7

things it might not be wise to discuss in front of the children. Longarm had naturally cuffed one of his prisoner's wrists to a handy brass rail of the bunk bed. So he simply nodded, and the two of them stepped out into the companionway for her to confide, "We should have gotten off back there when we had the chance. I know this line. There's nobody that can help him at that Gila Bend agency if it's his appendix. There's nobody anywhere who'll be able to save him if his appendix bursts before we get him to a real surgeon. What if we were to take him off at the next water stop and catch a westbound back to Yuma?"

To which Longarm could only reply with a sigh, "What westbound coming when, Miss Ilsa? They run passenger trains both ways at night across this desert in high summer. Next westbound for Yuma will just be leaving Deming with a good twelve-hour run ahead of her."

She made a wry face and decided, "We'd be far better off holding out for Deming and hoping for the best then. They'd never be able to help him at the Gila Bend agency, and poor old Doctor Wolfram at Growler Wash just doesn't have the sanitary facilities for any really serious operation."

She turned to go back into the compartment. But Longarm reached out to stop her, saying, "Hold on, ma'am. You say there's a *surgeon* at that flag stop way this side of Gila Bend?"

She nodded, but said, "Retired. Seventy years old and trying to grow olives, dates, or something on an experimental farm near that trading post and desert post office. We don't want to get off *there* with poor Mister Drake and an inflamed appendix! They say Doctor Wolfram was a wonder at saving limbs when he was running that Union field hospital in his salad days. But even if he still has his old skills, the risky operation that may be called for is a whole new procedure and, as I just said, old Doctor Wolfram is running an experimental farm, not a modern hospital, so . . ."

Longarm slid the compartment door open to call in to the conductor, "Could you stop this train and let the three of us off at Growler Wash, pard?"

The conductor replied, "I command this fool train. I can stop it anywhere I've a mind to. But why would anyone want to get off at that cluster of 'dobes around our railroad trestle in the middle of nowhere, after sundown, during an Apache scare?"

Longarm explained, "Sister Anders here knows a retired surgeon there."

The prisoner melting ice on the bunk with his warm belly moaned, "I don't want no *retired* sawbones touching my fair white body! I want to go to that hospital in Deming you were talking about before. Then I want another doctor to look at me before anyone cuts into me. For I have heard it said that opening up a man's belly can be perilous as all get-out!"

Longarm didn't answer. He read enough to know Drake was only repeating common medical opinion. Thanks to modern painless surgery, opening up the skull, chest, or abdominal cavity was now more possible. But it was improbable that the patient would recover from the almost sure-to-fester incisions and sutures. It would have been unkind to tell a convicted killer what the exact odds were. So he simply let the nurse assure Drake nobody was about to cut him open if there was any other way to keep his fool appendix from busting inside him like an overstuffed sausage. Longarm had read how some docs held it was best to open and clean out the ruptured guts as a last resort, while some few others were in favor of going in ahead of time, removing the swollen appendix in one piece *before* it burst, and hoping plenty of phenol and prayer as you backed out of the exposed innards would offer a better hope against infection.

Sister Ilsa allowed strong liquor wasn't likely to put Drake in any more peril than he seemed to be in. So Longarm had that dining car attendant fetch them a bottle of Maryland Rye. The conductor only stayed for one swig before he had to move on with his ticket puncher, assuring them he'd let them off at Growler Wash unless they changed their minds. So Harmony Drake got to swallow most of the pint, with Longarm and the gal helping, as the train crawled on through a desert night with plenty of stars but no moon worth mentioning.

Longarm knew the flag stop the nurse had mentioned lay about half way between Yuma and Gila Bend. So he wasn't surprised less than two hours later to feel the train was slowing down. He was on his own feet and had his prisoner dressed more modestly, uncuffed from the bunk bed, when the conductor came back to say they were fixing to stop and to ask about their baggage.

The gal said her one overnight bag had been checked through to Deming and that she figured she might as well pick it up from their depot once she got there.

Longarm said his prisoner had no baggage, and allowed he'd trust the same railroad with his own light baggage, seeing they'd all be going to the end of the line shortly if Doc Wolfram could do something for Harmony Drake's indisposition. He felt no call to discuss funeral arrangements in front of any man before he was sure they'd be needed.

So with Drake allowing that he was starting to feel better, thanks to all that ice, or Maryland Rye, they got him out on the car platform by the time their train rattled across a trestle spanning a wide dry wash and hissed to a stop on the far side, with a handful of window lights watching them from the low starlit adobes of the desert hamlet.

Some dimly lit figures commenced to drift toward them as Longarm and the gal helped the gimpy Harmony Drake down the steps to the trackside gravel. Sister Ilsa called out for help in getting a mighty sick man over to Doctor Wolfram's place. After some buzzing back and forth, one of the hands allowed in a friendly tone that he knew who they were talking about. So it seemed as if they all wanted to help as the conductor up on the platform yanked his bell cord and the night train proceeded onward up the line.

Longarm asked which way they were trying to herd his sick prisoner, seeing they seemed to be milling nowhere in particular, even with the tracks cleared and nothing blocking progress in any fool direction.

Then somebody drove another night train right against the back of Longarm's skull, and he just had time to gasp, "Gee, Doc, I thought she was a *nice* gal," before this inkwell opened wide and swallowed him lock, stock, and barrel.

Chapter 2

After he'd been at it a spell, Longarm got to wondering why he was soaring through the night like an owl-bird with a headache, high above the stars. Then it came to him that he was looking up, not down, at the starry desert sky and that his only resemblance to any species of bird was that he seemed to be lying spread-eagle on his back as naked as a jay.

He naturally tried to do something about that, and decided to stop and think some more when somebody drove a red hot hat pin into his bare back. For the sons of bitches had staked him by his wrists and ankles aboard an ant pile, and this was no time to wake a million or more red harvesters from their evening repose!

The night air all around was goose-pimple cold by now. It wouldn't warm enough to really stir the multitudes just under him before the sun rose a bit. But once you sorted all those stars into constellations, they read that it was well past midnight. That meant he had four to six hours to bust loose, without busting more of the crust he lay upon. They'd left him a swell choice. He could relax and just wait to be eaten alive after sunrise, or invite thousands of tiny venomous jaws to enjoy him as a late-night snack by straining at his bonds!

As he lay there considering his grim options, he became aware of a dark figure standing over what would be the head of his grave if the bastards had had the common courtesy to just gun a man and bury him. After a spell, Longarm croaked, "Howdy, you son of a bitch. I hope you'll forgive my not rising."

There came no answer. Longarm called his mysterious tormentor a mighty *silly* son of a bitch, adding, "Shoot and be damned, you asshole. The show you're waiting to see don't start until well after sunrise, and I hope they bite you too!"

Then, as he gingerly craned his neck for a better look, he saw that the Milky Way sort of outlined one of the figure's shoulders, if it had had a real shoulder. Then the pattern fell in place and Longarm marveled, "Now why would they have wanted to strip me bare-ass, then hang my duds on cross sticks like they were building a damned old scarecrow?"

His head still throbbed, but it was working better now, so before long he decided, "Right. It's far more noticeable from a passing train. Billy Vail sent me all the way to Arizona to transport a paid assassin with an escape-artist rep. So Drake and his pals knew full well that as soon as I didn't come back to Denver with him, Denver would come looking for me and him."

His duds didn't even flutter in the chill night air.

Longarm almost shrugged before he remembered all those tiny jaws under him. "They slickered me in a way that makes Samson in the Good Book look like a suspicious banker," he continued out loud. "At least he got to *lay* Miss Delilah before she made a chump out of him. So they had to know I worked for a smarter lawman, and we all heard that conductor commenting on the three of us getting off here."

An August meteor shot across the Milky Way on high. So Longarm made the only sensible wish a man in his position could think of, and added aloud, "The all-points Billy Vail sends out by wire will trace the three of us this far. That conductor warned us about Victorio's band being off the reservation this summer. Victorio ain't about to lead his bronco bunch west betwixt the Fourth Cav at Fort Apache and the Sixth Cav at Fort Huachuca, even in cooler weather. But how many white eyes *know* this, and what are they likely to say when they find yours truly eaten alive on an ant pile Apache style, with my prisoner and a pretty white gal missing? Would *you* want to trail bronco Apache across this desert in high summer when everyone but the army agrees it's a proper chore for the damned old army?"

He reflected nobody who'd seen him getting off that train with what seemed a sick prisoner and a nursing sister would be in any position to describe anyone else. But that line of reasoning only worked if Drake's pals had wiped out even the modest population of a small flag stop.

"I'm sorry, Victorio," Longarm muttered aloud. "Some of my own kind can beat any Indian born at thinking mean, and you're still likely to get blamed for another one of your famous massacres here."

Then he heard a soft female voice call out, " *'Onde esta, El Brazo Largo?''*

Since Brazo Largo meant Longarm in Border Spanish, the tied-down man so addressed was inspired to quietly call back, "*Aqui. Quien es?*"

Then a small dark angel of mercy who smelled just awful hunkered over him with the starlight gleaming on the keen blade of her barlow knife. When Longarm warned her about the ants, she said she knew. She'd heard those *ladrones* laughing about what they were planning to do to him long before they'd done it.

His dusky rescuer worked gently and carefully on the rawhide the sons of bitches had bound him with. So he only got bitten on the bare ass one time as she helped him roll free of the sleepy but pissed-off ant pile. He grabbed his duds and got them well clear of the milling red ants. They'd stolen his six-gun, badge, and identification, along with his watch and derringer. But he was mildly surprised to discover they'd left him his Stetson and stovepipe army boots, as well his tweed pants, long underwear, and hickory shirt.

As he hunkered amid stickerbrush to cover his nakedness, he learned the gal answered to Rosalinda. She said she spoke more English than the pals of Harmony Drake had thought. So once she'd heard them discussing their plans for *her*, she'd hidden out a full day in the last place a stranger to such parts might think to look.

An August afternoon on the flat roof of a 'dobe trading post, listening to them talking about you below, accounted for the poor little thing's dire need of a bath. She and her sweated-up cotton shift now reeked with the combined odors of mesquite smoke, 'dobe dust, and armpit all over.

Once he was dressed, although flat broke and without a weapon to his name, Rosalinda led him toward the only lamplight left, explaining how *los ladrones* had lit candle stubs all about to make the deserted flag stop seem more lively. She said she'd put them out to prevent the place from going up in flames as she'd heard them intending.

As they got to the trading post door she'd left ajar, Longarm saw an arrow stuck in the jam. It might have struck him as more artistic if it hadn't been one of those gussied-up toy arrows they made to sell tourists along the railroad lines.

He wrinkled his nose and said, "It's nice to know they're capable of *some* mistakes. That blonde they had laying for me on the night train from Yuma was too slick for this child by half! She forced a card on me, like a tinhorn dealing to a greenhorn! *I* was the one insisting on getting *off* here! They must have been laughing like hell as they rode

15

off with my badge, my other stuff, and my prisoner!''

She said they surely had been as she led him inside, waving at the trade goods scattered carelessly and the candle stub set in a pile of tinder under a wall shelf as she explained, ''As I told you, they did not know I spoke English, or that I was right above their heads as they were plotting. I knew who you were as soon as I heard one of them say they could sell your pistol and identification in Sonora to *los rurales*. Everyone this close to the border knows of the reward on the head of El Brazo Largo.''

He asked her to rein in and start at the beginning. So she did, and she was interesting to look at too as she told her sad, simple story.

Longarm figured her for a Mexican-Papago breed of nineteen at the most. For the slight waves in her dusty black hair spoke Spanish, and while her pretty little heart-shaped face spelled Papago, she still had her short but ample figure.

The desert-dwelling Papago nation offered living proof that old Professor Darwin might have been on to something with that notion of flora, fauna, and folks evolving to fit their ways of life. It was easy to see by their blossoms how the desert cactus plants had started out as some kin to the rosebush, forced to get by in country too dry for any regular rose. The Papago had likely begun as plain old Indians. But a heap of living where the living was hard on a jackrabbit had produced a breed of short wiry folks who could thrive on next to nothing, or bloat up like a circus fat lady if they dared to eat half as much as anyone else—Anglo, Mex, or even Pueblo.

As if to prove Professor Darwin's point, Rosalinda rummaged amid the spilled trade goods for something to eat as she told him how she and her two sisters, the daughters of a Butterfield wrangler and his Indian *mujer*, had all three married up with the Anglo trader here at Growler Wash, a nice old Mormon gent called Pop Wolfram.

Longarm forced himself not to cut in. It was obvious that

that so-called nurse aboard the train had been making up her retired surgeon in this dying settlement. Rosalinda went on to explain how the real Wolfram had set up this trading post when the Butterfield coaches still had a relay stage there, where the east-west stage line crossed a north-south desert trail up Growler Wash from the Gila Flats to the north.

Traveling by coach across the southwest corner of Arizona Territory had never been a pleasure. So travelers and even the U.S. Mail had given it up entirely when the new rail line between Yuma and Deming had followed the same route across the burning wastes. To say business had been slow at an abandoned Butterfield relay station and occasional flag stop would be to imply you didn't sell much soda pop in a graveyard.

One of Rosalinda's sisters and co-wives had gone off to live back on the blanket with Indian kin. Rosalinda and a more optimistic older sister had hung on, hoping things would pick up. When they hadn't, her husband and elder sister had left Rosalinda in charge and flagged a train to Yuma, in hopes of finding a buyer for all this unsold merchandise.

Rosalinda said she'd been waiting there alone for the better part of a week when four riders had come along the tracks one early morn, leading two more saddle mounts and four pack mules.

She said that when one of them addressed her in Spanish, she'd been smart enough to reply in the same, not letting on that she followed their drift as they said mean things about her tits in English.

As she and Longarm sipped pork and beans from the cans as if it was thick soup, cow-camp style, Rosalinda asked with a pouty face if he thought her *chupas* were too big for the rest of her. He assured her she had *chupas muy linda*, and asked her to go on.

She said the riders had begun by helping themselves to

17

three mules' worth of trail supplies, with the one speaking Spanish making up a big fib about paying up as they were leaving. She'd figured what the payoff was likely to be when one of them sniggered in English about her great little *culo*. So she'd drifted out back as if headed for the outhouse. Then she'd swiftly climbed a pole ladder to the flat roof and pulled it up after her. She started to explain how she and her sisters had often cooled off up yonder on straw matting after a long hot day. But Longarm bade her to stick to the mystery riders.

So she did, and it was soon less mysterious. They'd yelled back and forth when they'd searched in vain for her outside. And then she'd been listening at the stovepipe through the clay and matting roof as they'd whiled away a whole day waiting for Longarm, a pal called Harmony, and a slick-talking gal called Goldmine Gloria.

When she got that far, Longarm put down his empty can and groaned, "Oh, Lord, I'll never live this down! I've read the fliers out on a confidence gal called Goldmine Gloria Weaver, and I let her force cards on me anyway! You say your man and older sister caught the train to Yuma about a week ago, Miss Rosalinda?"

She nodded and sighed, "I fear they never meant for to come back. Papa always liked fat Maria best. She is willing for to do things my other sister and me find *perverso*. Is harder for even a Mormon to get by with more than one *mujer* in California, no?"

Longarm said soberly, "They might not have made it that far. A killer called Harmony Drake was arrested in Yuma just ten days ago. If pals who were still at large sent for Goldmine Gloria right after, she could have been on the night train from Deming when it stopped around dawn for your man and your sister. They call her Goldmine Gloria because she makes friends fast aboard trains, with a view to selling a gold mine, water rights, or whatever. It wouldn't have taken such a slick talker long to sense the

18

golden opportunity her newly made friends from Growler Wash were offering her on a silver platter.''

He shook his head wearily and added, ''And I was the one who insisted we get off here, like that fly stepping into the parlor of that spider!''

There was a brass alarm clock ticking on a shelf near the emptied cash till. If it was halfway right, they had a little over two hours' wait for that train down from Deming. Meanwhile the outlaws would be riding south along a goose-pimple-cool trail, and they'd likely make a few more miles before it warmed up enough to matter after sunrise.

He added the travel times in his head and groaned aloud. ''I don't see how I can make it come out right. Say we get in to Yuma early in the morning and I have no trouble rounding up a federal posse. Say the next train back leaves earlier than usual tomorrow evening, and we cut their trail in the dark with no trouble. The border lies, what, sixty-odd miles, or two nights of hard riding, from here?''

She nodded, cheerfully considering, and said you followed the flats west of the Growler Range as far as Organpipe Pass, then punched through a cactus jungle astride the unguarded border, and then it was almost all downhill to the Sea of Cortez and a steamboat out to most anywhere.

Longarm swore under his breath and decided, ''Way too tight. I have orders not to cross the border anymore, and I'd play hell getting more fussy lawmen to ride into Sonora with me. Can you think of anywhere closer I could come by a pony or, better yet, a riding mule, ma'am?''

She said her other sister had been able to walk home to her maternal kin holed up for the summer in a nearby canyon. She added that her uncle, as close to being a chief as the free and easy Papago would abide, kept a remuda of riding stock. Then she spoiled it all by pointing out how Longarm would be riding after those *ladrones* alone and unarmed.

He muttered, ''When you're right you're right, ma'am.

I don't suppose you'd have anything like a shooting iron for sale around here.''

She shook her dusty head and said those pals of Harmony Drake had even helped themselves to most of the ammunition they'd had in the store.

A less experienced questioner might have let that one word get past him. But Longarm brightened and asked, "You said *most*, Miss Rosalinda?"

She shrugged her tawny shoulders under her filthy thin shift and moved around the end of the counter to produce a couple of brick-sized cardboard boxes as she told him *los ladrones* had laughed to see them on sale.

Longarm smiled thinly and said he could see why they hadn't bothered to steal the ammunition. He asked, "How come you stock buffalo rounds down here where the jackrabbit and Gila monster roams?"

She said there were mule deer over in the Growlers, and then recalled one of those Butterfield hands across the way had kept an old single-shot hunting rifle.

Since she'd already told him about that outfit pulling up stakes and moving on, he came close to letting it go at that. But they paid Longarm to be nosy. So he was, and she recalled they'd been stuck with over a hundred rounds of .50-120-600 when the old-fashioned coot across the way had come down with the ague and died on the job.

Longarm bent to snatch that unlit candle stub from the floor as he asked if she could spare him some matches and show him around the abandoned stage stop.

She said she could, but being a woman, pestered him all the way across the dusty road about his eccentric taste in rifle-guns. She said, "Even if you find the *pobrecito*'s old gun, you do not wish for to go after five *hombres* and a dangerous *mujer* with a single-shot weapon, do you?"

To which he could only reply, "They don't pay me to do what I *want*, and the only rifle chambered .50-120-600 is that Sharps '74 Big Fifty. I'll allow it takes forever to load a Big Fifty next to, say, a Winchester or even a Spencer. But once she's loaded, watch out!''

They found another dumb arrow stuck on the open door across the way. Rosalinda said she'd noticed the silly toy when she'd darted all over to snuff all those candles.

Longarm lit the candle he was packing just inside the door, and saw how the Butterfield outfit had left the heavy plank tables and benches in the dining room so those fake Indian raiders could tip them over.

The office next door was empty, save for old papers strewn across the dirt floor. Longarm nodded at the snuffed-out candle amid a pile of crumpled paper in one corner, and said, ''That wouldn't have done a whole lot, even if you hadn't nipped it on the bud. These thick 'dobe walls are sort of tough to set afire.''

Then he noticed something black and limp as the skin of a witch's cat draped over a corner of the windowsill. When he picked it up he saw it was a gal's fancy black lace chemise. He sniffed it and said, ''Brand-new, never worn, and meant to be found. Reckon Goldmine Gloria wanted to be remembered as a gal who'd been wearing clean and classy unmentionables when those red devils dragged her fair white body off to a fate worse than death.''

Rosalinda gasped. ''*Ay, que lujoso*! Is that real French *encaje*?''

Longarm handed the frilly underwear to her, saying, ''Goldmine Gloria seems a real spender, considering how honestly she comes by her money.''

The little breed gal held the black lace as if she feared it was a fragile treasure as she gasped, ''Is for me? I can have it? *Muchas gracias*, and I can not wait for to put it on. *Pero* first I ought to take a bath, no?''

He allowed that seemed a sensible notion, and moved on, shielding the flickering candle flame with his free hand as they explored the cluttered 'dobe maze. He could sense the bitterness of the suddenly out-of-work coaching hands as they'd hurriedly packed to move on, traveling by the rails that were making long-distance coaching obsolete. Longarm considered himself as progressive as most, but you had to feel wistful for overnight old-timers in a rapidly changing West.

He murmured aloud, "Seems the old boys just got good at trapping beaver when it came time to hunt buffalo instead. Reckon the older hand who was working here when he died hunted buff before the Concord coach became the rage."

She told him the old man had been sort of silly to hunt rabbit with his old buffalo gun. She said, "Is not much meat on *el conejo* for to begin with."

Longarm grimaced at the mental picture, and agreed a Big Fifty was more gun than one needed to hunt skinny desert jacks.

But he was after bigger game. So he kept searching until he found it at last, wrapped in a dusty bedroll atop a wardrobe in one of the back bunk chambers.

He grinned wolfishly as he unwrapped the Sharps '74 .50-120-600, noting it had been cleaned and stored away with a thick coat of whale oil. The tooled steel of the sliding-block breech moved slick as silk, and the peep sights were set at five hundred yards, or close range for a Big Fifty. He turned to Rosalinda with a smile on his lips and death in his gun-muzzle gray eyes to ask her how far they had to walk to see her Papago kin about that riding stock.

She said, "No more than three hours, and will not be too hot for to walk before nine or ten in the morning. But those *ladrones* carry rifles too. *Repeating* rifles that go bang, bang, bang!"

Longarm patted the oiled steel of the Big Fifty and calmly informed her, "This artillery piece don't bang. She throws way better than two times the weight of a Winchester, more than three times as far, with the punch to stop full-grown buffalo."

Rosalinda shook her dusty head and pointed out, "One at a time. There are five of them. Six if you count that blond *puta*. What do you expect the others to do after you get off your single shot, hold their own fire as they patiently await their own turns for to die, *optomisto mio*?"

Chapter 3

The eastern sky was pearling pink behind the jagged black skyline of the Growler Range by the time Longarm had both Rosalinda and the Big Fifty atop the flat-roofed trading post with him.

She'd washed her tawny hide and wavy black hair with laundry soap and sprinkled herself with lilac water before slipping into that black lace chemise and nothing else. She seemed to feel well dressed for polite Papago society. Longarm had to allow she looked as fine as she smelled now.

While she'd been washing up, Longarm had busied himself choosing other stuff they'd need for desert travel. He'd left most of their supplies below, but hauled a canvas bandolier he'd loaded with Big Fifty cartridges topside, along with the gun they went with.

It had been some time since Longarm had handled an old buffalo gun. But there seemed to be no rush as, way off in the desert, the night train from Deming whistled something off the tracks.

He levered the sliding block down to expose the half-inch chamber. As he slid the monstrous brass cartridge in, Rosalinda was asking why they were waiting for the train up there. She explained, "When you wish for to stop a train at Growler Wash, you must stand by the tracks and *wave* something at it, *comprende*?"

Longarm levered the block back up to note with satisfaction how old Christian Sharps's simple but clever action snapped tight as any banker might want his money vault. Earlier breech-loaders had tended to leak hot gasses in a marksman's face. But the breech designed by old Christian sealed itself even tighter when pressure built up inside. That was why his guns could take ever grander loads of powder and ball, starting with the military round of seventy, then the original plains rifle round of ninety, and then on to this swamping 120 grains that lobbed a bullet farther than most men could aim, if the truth were to be told.

As he braced the loaded and locked rifle on the 'dobe parapet he told Rosalinda, "Ain't aiming to flag no train to Yuma. I want to see if anyone *else* crawls out of a hidey-hole to flag it down."

She asked, "Who could you be thinking of? I told you those *ladrones* were planning for to sell your badge and wallet south of the border, for the reward on El Brazo Largo!"

Longarm nodded grimly and replied, "Didn't you tell me you were a Papago? Ain't you never heard of a rabbit doubling back on its tracks? We don't have it in writing that all six of 'em were planning on such a long dusty ride."

Rosalinda pouted, "Had my mother wished for to raise us all on rabbit meat and cactus fruit, she would not have wed our Mexican papa. But I know how game doubles back for to fool the hunter. *Pero* for why have they not tried for to kill you some more if they did not ride off as we thought?"

Longarm said, "Like *you* thought, you mean. I'd want that flashy Goldmine Gloria out of my hair before I commenced to cross over the border and moseyed my gringo

25

way to a sleepy Mex seaport, no offense."

She told him he was even smarter than they said he was along that same border. She asked if it was true El Brazo Largo had once wiped out a Mexican Army artillery column over in the Baja.

He modestly allowed he'd had help, and added, "I get along with a few of the more decent Mex lawmen. They ain't all bad. Just the total *pendejo* running the country."

She agreed El Presidénte Diaz was *sin falta un chingado zorillo,* or a fucking skunk, and then they could see the smoke plume of the night train from Deming, puffing as if it really wanted to get to Yuma by sunrise.

Longarm full-cocked the Big Fifty and braced it across the 'dobe parapet they were hunkered behind as the train came into full view, going lickety-split and never slowing down as it rumbled across the trestle spanning Growler Wash.

Longarm put the hammer back on half-cock and decided, "Reckon they figured Goldmine Gloria would stand out less in Mexico than along a railroad line she's been known to frequent. You say your uncle's camp is about a three-hour walk?"

She said they had plenty of time for a hearty breakfast and some strong black coffee to get them off to a good start.

He started to argue. But she'd been letting him have a hell of a lot of stuff on easy credit, and he was counting on her goodwill to set him up with that Indian riding stock he couldn't pay for either. So he allowed he'd scout to the south for sign while she warmed up some more canned goods.

It was getting light enough to see colors now, so going down the ladder ahead of Rosalinda, lest she need some catching, was a tad tougher on his nerves than going up it had been. For that lace chemise covered her chunky brown thighs a third of the way down if you were standing beside her. But the view from below was more sassy, and it seemed to be true that Spanish ancestry made for more body hair than pure Indian.

But she was a married-up gal. Sort of. Longarm had long suspected Mormons and Indians got on better with one another than either could with Queen Victoria's crowd because they weren't as inclined to primp for their womenfolk.

It took a heap of flowers, books, and romantic twaddle to justify the warmer feelings a properly brought-up Eastern gal was expected to have for a weak-chinned banker's son instead of, say, a poor but honest cowhand or, hell, a good-looking blacksmith who didn't own his own business yet. Queens and such were expected to fall madly in love as diplomacy dictated, as if they were brood mares being paired with the proper stallion to drop foals with proper papers. So they had to get married in cathedrals with mile-long trains, organs blaring, bells ringing, and the multitude waving lest anybody wonder what in thunder the happy couple *saw* in one another.

Brother Brigham of the Latter-Day Saints had noticed while headed west that he had more women than men tagging along, and seeing that both the King James Good Book and that Book of Mormon encouraged folks to be fruitful and multiply, he'd revealed with little romantic blathering that it was all right for a man to marry up with all the wives who'd have him. The Indians wandering the western deserts had already come to much the same conclusion. But neither pragmatic bunch carried on as shockingly as some newspaper reporters alleged. Rape was almost unheard of among the Saints and their mostly Uto-Aztec-speaking neighbors, and while some parents were always inclined to marry off the daughter of the house to a rich old man, neither the Salt Lake Temple nor your average medicine man condoned the practice of making a maiden marry against her will, which was more than some royal families could say.

So it was safe to say Rosalinda and her sisters had married up with that missing Mormon trader fair and square for practical reasons. It was easy to see little Rosalinda had a healthier appetite than your average handsome Papago was ever going to satisfy.

As she whipped up her second breakfast before sunrise Longarm and the Big Fifty scouted out across the desert pavement to the south for sign. It was easy to find and easy to read as the first rays of sunrise caught everything at a low angle in golden and lavender tones. Desert pavement was what you got between the tall columns of cactus and low thorny scrub after the dry winds blew away all the fine dust and the mineral salts from deeper down were sucked to the surface by the rare rains to cement the fine pebble and coarse sand together. Mexicans called it caliche. By any name it formed a brittle surface, thick as cardboard that gave away the progress of any critter heavier than, say, a rat or lizard.

Exactly six steel-shod ponies and a couple of unshod and heavier-laden mules or smaller ponies had moved south the night before in a column of twos at a trot. Longarm made a mental note that for all her faults, the brassy Goldmine Gloria was a good rider. You ate more miles at a cool trot than at any other gait. But sissy riders of any gender found that the most uncomfortable way to ride. Experienced riders did too. But you called them experienced because they knew how to get the most mileage out of a horse. It helped some if you stood in the stirrups and only let the jiggedy jogging saddle spank you now and again.

Longarm turned and headed back to the trading post adding in his head. He knew experienced riders would still be moving at this hour, trotting two furlongs, walking one trail-breaking for, say, ten minutes out of every ninety, then slowing down to fifteen-or twenty-minute rests for each hour in the saddle as their confidence grew and their mounts got wearier. He knew an old-time Pony Express rider could have made it to the border by this time. But those hell-for-leather kids had gotten to change ponies every ten miles or so. Harmony Drake's bunch had to get sixty or more before they'd be out of his jurisdiction.

He nodded to himself and decided, "They'll play it cavalry style. They'll call thirty miles a fair ride and hole up for the day no more than halfway to the border. So if I head after them after sun down, the way I'm supposed to, they'll be crossing into Sonora about the time I find their damned midway camp at dawn!"

He stomped inside to find Rosalinda, naked as a jay, setting a plank kitchen table with their heroic breakfast.

She'd been enough to give a man pause in that black lace chemise. It hadn't half shown how flawless her smooth tawny charms really were. A lot of gals that were still worth screwing had protruding or otherwise odd belly buttons, mismatched nipples, and so on. But Rosalinda's casually displayed body was just plain perfection.

He tried not to comment as he sat down to inhale bully beef and tomato preserves with Arbuckle Brand coffee. But as she sat demurely bare-ass across from him, she felt obliged to tell him she'd stripped to keep from spattering her swell new dress.

Longarm laughed despite himself and said, "That black lace left behind as a red herring is meant to be worn as a *combinacíon*, not a *vestido* for street wear, Miss Rosalinda."

She nodded and said, "You told me. *Pero* I do not intend for to wear it on the streets of Yuma. I intend to wear it for Papago friends and relations to admire. Do you really think my *chupas* are too big? I see you avoid them with your eyes and I am not used to this. Even my poor old husband liked for to look at the three of us as we served him his morning coffee in bed."

Longarm sighed and said, "Ain't nothing wrong with your tits, Miss Rosalinda. It's just that you're a married-up

29

lady and . . . Hold on, did you say you and your sister served a Mormon *coffee* in bed, all three of you stark naked?''

She pouted. ''*Sí*. Then he asked us for to put on a naughty show for him. He was generous and kind, *pero* as I said, *old*. So perhaps he had trouble with his manhood and needed more *inspiración* than most. As I told you, Fat Maria was willing. *Pero* Felicidad and me felt it would be bad medicine, as well as a mortal sin, if two blood relatives did such things to one another while he and a third *mujer* went *reverso*.''

Longarm cut in with a laugh. ''Never mind the lip smacking details. A dirty old man pretending to be a Mormon should have known how most Indians would rather indulge in cannibalism than incest in any way, shape, or form. He had to be *pretending* to be a Mormon because whilst a real Latter-Day Saint might or might not make Indian wives wear that special Mormon underwear, he'd never let them serve him coffee, tea, or tobacco, in bed or anywhere *else*. How did he go about convincing the three of you he was marrying up with you according to the Book of Mormon?''

She looked blank, and then recalled the old trader had said something about writing their names in the flyleaf of his Good Book to make it all lawful and binding. Then she asked what was so funny.

He said, ''You ain't married up to nobody, Miss Rosalinda. If it's any comfort to you, Goldmine Gloria doubtless pulled the wool over his eyes as well on the way in to Yuma. I'll try to find out what happened to him and your elder sister when I catch up with the sass. So what say we quit messing around and get cracking!''

She said that sounded like a grand suggestion, and swept the tin cup and plates from the table to climb up on top of it and spread herself in wide welcome by the dawn's early light.

Longarm rose thoughtfully to his feet, unbuttoning his shirt, as he murmured, ''Well, as long as it's all in the line of duty . . .''

But he enjoyed it too, once he was pronging her hard and deep with his feet on the dirt floor, a palm braced atop the table to either side of her wriggling hips, and with her bare ankles over both his naked shoulders. For she was almost too tight for him, and he believed her when she bragged that she'd never had that much manhood inside her, or any man at all for some time. He told her she was built just right for him as well. So they naturally wound up back in her bedroom, and a good time was had by all as Rosalinda showed him what that imaginative old trader had wanted her to do with her sister. He had to allow it didn't seem as sinful, seeing she'd just had a bath and they weren't even distant cousins.

So between one swell position and another, it was broad daylight outside before they headed out, half satisfied and heavily laden, as the morning sun made short work of the cooling effects of that hot shower they'd enjoyed under cold water out back.

Longarm had suggested Rosalinda load up on gifts for her Papago kinfolk, seeing she'd be staying with them till it was safe for her and her one surviving sister at the trading post they likely now owned.

Aside from that Big Fifty and its bulky ammunition, Longarm knew how much more important water could be than other trail supplies in the country out ahead. So he helped himself to a couple of five-gallon water bags, but left them empty for now, with water weighing eight pounds a gallon and Rosalinda sure they could make her uncle's summer camp on a couple of canteens. Longarm slung the Big Fifty and bandolier of buffalo rounds across his chest, and shoved all the trail grub he had room for in the two gunnysacks he'd packed with water bags, flannel blankets, canvas tarps, and so on. Then he tied the ends of the two sacks together and slung the knot over his left shoulder to take the lead Indian style. Indian men didn't walk ahead of womankind to be rude. They considered it cowardly to let women and children stomp on the horse apples and rattle snakes ahead of them. They walked with no load but their weapons so they could spot trouble faster than a gal trudging head-down with all their baggage. But there was no way a gal as small as Rosalinda could have packed both their loads on a level walk, even on a cooler morning.

Longarm figured it was now somewhere in the eighties and he knew it would soon be a whole lot hotter. But with any luck they'd be able to make it by noon. Folks of any race along the border knocked off for *la siesta* by noon if they had a lick of sense and any reason to go on living. Folks from other parts were inclined to consider *la siesta* a lazy Latin habit. They were used to dividing their day up into hours set aside for working, resting, eating, sleeping, and so on. Both the Spanish-speaking folks and the desert dwellers knew better. Whether Moorish or American Indian, they divided their days up into times of being too hot or cool enough to move. This inspired them to keep hours others found odd. The same lazy-looking Mexican you'd find knocking off for the afternoon was likely to be open for business at midnight, or having a party at three in the morning. The hands of a man-made clock had less say than the rays of that ferocious sun up yonder in this part of the world.

But this early in the day, the southwest corner of Arizona Territory could get almost pretty in its own exotic way. Whether you called it the Yuma Desert or the northern reaches of the Sonora Desert, it was all trying to make up its mind whether it could best be described as lusher than usual desert or drier than usual chaparral. The flora and fauna of such long-established dry country had had time to adapt to it more ways than you saw in younger deserts. Cactus grew in all sizes and shapes, from bitty pincushions

32

to the tall skinny organpipes and far more impressive saguaro, looming all about like holdup victims in green Robin Hood outfits.

Vicious jumping cholla tried to look like a cross between a cactus and a crab-apple tree, as if tempting the unwary traveler to get too close. There was lots of prickle-pear, and the knee-high barrel cactus that could save your life if you ran out of water and didn't mind drinking what looked like warm spit and tasted like soapy dishwater. Wherever the cactus roots or flash-flood washes left room, you saw thin chaparral, or stickerbush, from *creosota* and catclaw to eight- or ten-foot whitebark and paloverde.

It was just as well the eggshell-white trail they were following got plenty of dappled shade as they trudged ever upwards to the jagged teeth of the Growler Range to the east. It was already warm enough for the snakes and lizards to have quit for the day. Here and there something rustled amid the stickerbrush as they passed. But the only critters to be seen were buzzards and white-trimmed chocolate-dipped birds about the size and flocking habits of common crows. Rosalinda called them *halcones*. He had no call to argue with her, seeing she hailed from the same country as the big brown birds. But they didn't look like hawks to a West-by-God-Virginia boy.

He figured they'd walked about six country miles when they came to a dip, shaded by whitebark and carpeted with creeping thyme. Rosalinda dropped her own load and threw herself full length on the soft sweet-scented herbage, declaring she needed a rest but wouldn't be too averse to some gentle screwing in such a *romantico* setting.

Longarm was legsore enough to put down his load and prop the Big Fifty in a fork of whitebark. But even as he flopped down beside her, he said, "It's fixing to get hotter before it gets any cooler, *querida*. It ain't that I don't admire the way you're smiling up at me from under the hem of that scandalous lace chemise, but we just don't have the time!''

She rolled over on her hands and knees with the lacy hem all the way up around her waist as she pouted, ''Just one *chingita* before we get to my uncle's band, *por favor*. Is impossible to do in daylight without making the children laugh and point the fingers.''

Longarm was sorely tempted. Most men would have been. But it was going on 9:30 or later, and they had a ways to go before that August sun rose high enough to bake their brains inside their skulls on the open trail. He said so, as Rosalita wiggled her bare brown behind and moaned over her shoulder, like an alley cat in heat, that she'd settle for two fingers if he was feeling too *flojo* to do it right.

He laughed despite himself and said, ''It's tempting enough just *looking* at it, as well you know. But *sin falta, mi corazón,* the two of us are fixing to wind up with heat stroke if we don't make it to that canyon by high noon!''

She shook her head, tossing her unbound brunette waves as she insisted, ''*Pero no*. Is going for to rain this afternoon. Clouds will shade the trail ahead for us by the time you satisfy me. *Metetelo al funciete* and *satisfy* me if you are in so much of a hurry!''

Longarm tried to ignore the pressure inside his pants as he gaped up at the clear blue desert sky and demanded, ''How did you come up with that grand notion, *querida*? I've heard tell of wishful thinking, and it ain't that I don't wish we had the time, but . . .''

''*Ay, gringo mio*,'' she cut in. ''Did nobody ever tell you for to watch the birds along the trail?''

Longarm swept the clear sky with his keen eyes as he mused, half to himself, ''I don't see any birds up yonder at the moment.''

Then the penny clinked inside the player piano, and as the old song began to tinkle, he nodded at the only bird in sight, a distant buzzard perched atop a tall green saguaro, and decided, "Right. Birds don't fly as much when they sense a sudden change in the weather. You get your summer rains from the south-west in these parts, right?"

She moaned, "*Es verdad*. Take off your clothes. Put them away if you wish for to wear them dry this evening. Then put it in *me* and make us both sweat a lot, so we can really enjoy the cold shower we are in for whether we are entwined in *el rapto supremo* or not!"

Chapter 4

The Sonora Desert was unusually hot and dry because it was usually cut off from the Pacific westerlies by the coast ranges on the far side of the Colorado-Gila Delta. It was unusually green for a desert because from time to time it paid host to wet contrary winds from the Sea of Cortez or Gulf of California to the southwest. When it did this it got a lot of tropical rain all at once, along with downright dangerous thunder and lightning. So Longarm and Rosalinda were fairly sated by the time the desert downpour ended. For the reverends who advised horny young gents to take cold showers for their hard-ons had never showered with as horny a pal as Rosalinda, and every time the lightning had flashed it had inspired her already tight charms to clamp down like a hot, slick hangman's noose while they both wallowed in slippery mud and warm pounding rain.

The sun came back out to dry their hides and freshly laundered duds as they strolled on, naked as Adam and Eve before the Fall, had Adam been packing a Big Fifty along with his burlap sacks and such.

Where desert pavement lay flat, the rainwater was already getting blotted up by a root jungle that would have made Professor Darwin hug himself with glee. Stickerbush and cactus could grow closer to each other than either could abide neighbors of its own breed. The cactus roots spread far and wide but shallow, while the *creosota* and mesquite reached way down deep for water the cactus had failed to sop up near the surface.

Cactus got by between rains by storing water above-ground in its green pulp. In a wet year, such as this one, cactus could overindulge. It was usually too *much* water that ended the otherwise long and uneventful life of a tall saguaro. As Longarm and Rosalinda passed close by a couple, they could see the pleated thorny trunks were already commencing to bloat like the arms and legs of untended battlefield casualties, and by the day's end Longarm knew more than one ancient saguaro would have split its thorny green hide, like a kid grown too big for his britches, to expose its vulnerable juicy pulp to all the thirsty critters, large and small, who lay in wait all around for such rare treats.

Somewhere in the hazy blue-green distance they heard a long groan and the muffled crash of something big and soft smashing brittle dry branches. Rosalinda said, "Hohokam. They do that sometimes when it has been raining."

Longarm frowned thoughtfully and said, "We'd best stop here and put our duds back on. I thought that was a water-logged saguaro just now. Ain't Hohokam what your Papago kinfolk call the old time pueblo farmers who dug all those canals across a desert that must have been a tad less arid in their day?"

Rosalinda paused to take her black lace chemise from one of her own sacks as she explained. "Hohokam is difficult for to explain in Spanish or English. My mother's people do not always *think* a word as you Saltu, Anglo or Mexican, *say* it. Is bad medicine for to say *muerto* or *dead* in the tongue you call Papago. Hohokam may be thought as 'all used up' or 'those who have gone before us,' *comprende*?"

Longarm hunkered to remove his boots and put on his underwear as he replied with a dubious frown, "I ain't sure I do. I know the folks we think of as Apache or Navajo call the old-timers who left ruins up in *their* neck of the woods Anasazi. They seem unclear if they mean Ancient Enemies or just Old Timers when they call 'em Anasazi. I can't say I ever heard a Navajo call a dying cactus an Anasazi, though."

As he pulled his boots back on over his long underwear and pants, the part-Indian gal half-concealed her tawny charms in black lace as she explained, "Saguaros used to be people and still have spirits, don't they? You Saltu sometimes use the manlike saguaro for target practice, or even rope one and pull it over, for no reason. But Papago respect and honor them because they live longer than most grandmothers and give sweet red fruit for to eat or make wine, if you ask them politely."

Longarm buttoned his shirt and nodded, saying, "I follow your drift. Sort of. What say we push on to see if your alive and kicking kin can fix this child up with some riding stock."

They could, once you got them calmed down.

The almost childishy friendly Papago greeted Longarm as well as Rosalinda like long-lost kissing cousins they'd never expected to see alive again. They both were relieved of their bundles and escorted up a brush-choked canyon an outsider might have ridden past without even smelling a fair-sized but scattered encampment. The Papago were shy, as well as near-naked drifters.

Like their more settled Pima cousins, the Ho- or Uto-Aztec-speaking Papago might have been more famous and rated more chapters in the history books if they hadn't been such neighborly sorts. For they had to be sharp to get by in such grim country, and nobody who'd ever made the mistake of messing with them ever called them cowards.

The Pima and Papago bands of the Sonora Desert were the only nations both the Na-déne, or Apache, and ferocious Yaqui, or Unreconstructed Aztec, had long since learned to leave the hell alone. For grim tales were still told of the time Chiricahua raiders from the far-away White Mountains had hit the shyly smiling Papago for fun and ponies.

The Papago had followed the Apache raiders all the way home, like shadows, to pick them off one by one along the trail and then go on terrorizing them and their families, on their home ground, by cutting throats in bed and stabbing the backs of those on the way to take a pee. Their upset Enemies, for that was what "Apache" meant in Ho, tried to make peace by howling into the darkness and leaving presents for the shadowy Papago lurking all about like slick old timber wolves. But the Papago just went on patiently killing the Apache raiders, then their women, their children, and their dogs, until nothing was left of them. Then all the Papago had gone home to do a little farming and a lot of hunting and gathering in their own stark country, where the Apache never bothered them again. Those few Mexicans or Anglos who knew anything at all about the secretive desert dwellers left them alone for much the same reason. There was no great profit in raiding such humble folk to start with, and once you *did* raid them, they'd follow you all the way home to Mexico or, hell, Chicago or Saint Lou, according to some old-timers who'd bothered to break bread with the little rascals.

Longarm had broken bread with them in the past, and in that odd way illiterate cultures had of spreading the word, he was known far and wide among various Ho-speaking nations as Saltu ka Saltu, or "the stranger who is no stranger."

So Rosalinda's maternal uncle and traditional guardian knew who Longarm was as soon as his sister's child, and hence a woman of the same ancestry, introduced them in his smoky brush wickiup. It was just as well the older man, called Pogamogan, spoke fair Spanish. For Longarm knew they were being offered something to eat when the old Papago said something about *duka*, and everyone knew you said *ei* for yes and *ka* for no. But after that the lingo got awesomely tough to follow.

It started to rain some more as Longarm told Pogamogan and some of the other elders his sad story, seated cross-legged with a gourd bowl of blue-corn, nopal, and chili mush in his lap. Being a woman, even if she was blood kin, Rosalita and her older sister had naturally been sent off to eat and gossip somewhere else. Papago respected womankind, and never hit kids just for acting like kids. But they held it was as tough for men to talk around womankind as it was under a tree full of jaybirds.

When Longarm got to the part about being willing to sign a government IOU for the riding stock he needed to carry himself and the old Big Fifty after his prisoner and those other outlaws, Pogamogan's basalt eyen filled with tears and he sobbed in Spanish, "You enter my camp with a kinswoman you have rescued from bandits, you accept food and shelter from me, and then you imply I am a poor shit who must be paid for mere mules?"

Longarm soberly replied, "I was wrong and I know it. But it is the custom of my own chief that I take nothing without offering to pay for it."

Pogamogan snapped, "We are not agency people. We have never lived on your Great Father's blanket and we do not beg for salt and matches as children beg for . . . how do you say *penat* in Saltu?"

Longarm thought and decided *miel*, the Spanish for honey, was what they were groping for.

The graying Papago shrugged his leathery shoulders and declared, "We agree on what is in my heart. I will give you all the ponies or mules you think you need. But how do you expect to catch up with all those bad Saltu on this

40

side of the border? They have had all of this time to get away from you!''

Longarm swallowed a polite bite of mush, shook his head, and told Pogamogan, "I doubt they have more than a twelve-hour lead. Stubborn or desperate human beings can push themselves harder than anyone can get a pony or even a mule to move. They rode out of Growler Wash well after dark. Say they pushed on into the morning, and even allow they were smart as your niece about the weather. They'd have still had to hole up somewhere to let their riding stock recover. So even as we're talking about 'em, they're bedded down in some cactus flat or chaparral patch as their ponies browse and laze, no?''

The man who knew this country better consulted with his fellow elders in their chanting way before he turned back to Longarm to say, "You may be right. They may be holed up halfway to the border. This heavy rain will have smoothed over their sign. Even if you cut their trail, you will be moving on by sundown. If they ride no faster than your blue sleeves on patrol, they will be south of the un-guarded border before you could catch up with them.''

He glanced at the bandolier of cartridges across Long-arm's shirtfront and added with a sigh, "Perhaps this is just as well. By your own account, they overpowered you when you were wearing a six-shooter and carrying a double der-ringer. I think you would do well to leave them to the unsettled conditions in the even more dangerous desert to the south. We are desert dwellers and we would not go south of Organpipe Pass this summer. That Apache, raiding further east, has the Mexican *federales* out in force. So naturally the Yaqui are out on the warpath. *Los federales* simply can not ride past a pig, a chicken, or a pretty girl without molesting them.''

Longarm shrugged and replied, "I'll cross that border when I come to it. Right now I'm planning on beelining along the foothills with a couple of good riding mules in hopes of heading those outlaws off at Organpipe Pass. You're right about it being a waste of time if I scouted for sign after all this rain. I figure it's going to rain some more before sundown. They have a woman as well as more delicate mounts under the canvas I'm hoping they've spread across some handy branches. I'm hoping they're feeling as sure as you gents that they've gotten away clean, with more worries ahead than behind them.''

He got to work on his mush, knowing he was expected to clean the bowl if he knew what was good for him. Pogamogan chanted with others for a spell, then turned back to Longarm to say, "We have decided you really are a *saltu ka saltu*. You might beat them to the border, and it is true you are carrying a medicine gun. You may kill two or more of them before the others circle in and finish you off with repeating rifles. Organpipe Pass is not the narrow defile you may be picturing. It is no more than an easier route winding through rolling hills that are overgrown with organpipe, a *lot* of organpipe. So there is plenty of cover for men on foot with repeating rifles, coming at you from as many directions as there may be enemies determined for to kill you!''

Longarm gulped down a heroic mouthful of mush and swallowed a time or two before he calmly replied, "I've played tag in a cactus patch before. I could tell you a tale about evading Yaqui in a pear flat a spell back, but I don't like to brag. I don't suppose that any of you might have an old Spencer rifle or a Walker Colt you could spare me, though?''

Pogamogan morosely replied, "I was asking that just now. We prefer to hunt with bows and arrows we can make ourselves. We hunt no game a well-placed arrow will not bring down, and once the Saltu traders have you dependent on them for matches, salt, and gunpowder, you may as well put on a dog collar and hand them your leash.''

Longarm swallowed some more, nodded gravely, and soberly said he'd heard tell of those prospectors who'd trifled with a Papago maiden up along the Gila, only to wind up looking a lot like pincushions.

He added, "I've often wished I was as good with a bow and arrow as a rifle. Your point about rolling your own ammunition is well taken. But I've never had time for serious violin lessons either. So I'll have to do what I have to do with this old buffalo rifle."

He licked the last green scrap of nopal off his fingers to display refined desert manners, and added, "My Papago uncle has filled my belly to the bursting point. Would he and his brothers be offended if I only had cheroot tobacco to offer?"

Pogamogan showed he was a genuine gentleman by shaking his head with a thin smile and replying, "The offer is enough when a serious man with a good heart has said more than once that he is in a hurry. Come with me and choose the mules you wish for to ride on with. You won't ever head those enemies off at Organpipe Pass unless you leave right now, by a foothill trail we can show you, chanting for rain, a lot of rain."

Longarm rose to follow the older man outside, with an anxious glance at the sky. It was starting to look pretty, damn its cauliflower-head clouds swirled around in a cobalt-blue bowl by stirring-rods of sunbeam.

As he legged it up the brushy canyon after Pogamogan, rifle slung and packing his heavy burlap sacks, he heard a distant mutter of mountain thunder and grinned. He could almost hear the conversation in that far-off outlaw camp. Some would be for pushing on with the afternoon just right for riding. But older and wiser trail hands would be pointing out that the storm front was far from blown over and you could never rest a mount too much for a serious uphill dash for Sonora, another twenty or more miles ahead.

Like the Papago encampment itself, their remuda of over a hundred head had been hidden up a side canyon, watered by a recently dammed pool, with plenty of thorny but tasty mesquite for the ponies, mules, and burros to browse as a couple of Indian kids kept watch at the mouth of the natural stock pen.

Longarm told the older man he'd trust him to choose the mules. So it only took a few minutes before they were loading a matched pair of Spanish cordovans to move out.

Asking Papago for regular saddles would have made as much sense as asking them to supply him with a Gatling gun. Some horse nations made or stole fair saddles and bridles. Papago were still in the earlier stages of what was still a white man's notion, for all the bullshit about natural red horsemanship. So while the Indians helped Longarm fill his heavy water bags and lash them aboard one mule with *mecates* of braided horsehair, along with his other trail supplies, he knew he was expected to ride the other one bareback and to hell with the seat of his pants.

Both mules were outfitted with *jaguima* or hackamore halters, made of heavier braided rawhide, with a thick *bozal* or nose-pincher instead of a bit. Papago fought dragoon style, riding only to the scene of battle, then dismounting to fight on foot. So such simple rigs were all they bothered with, and what the hell, neither mule had ever had a steel bit between its teeth, and this would hardly be the time to retrain either.

So he accepted the long lead line with a nod of thanks, and forked himself and the Big Fifty aboard the other mule. He'd been braced for Pogamogan to ask him if he wanted to say adios to Rosalinda. Mexicans would have considered him a shit to just ride off on a gal like that. But with any luck Rosalinda was thinking more Indian now that she'd spent some time with her mother's kinfolk. Longarm tended to agree with most Indians that long tearful good-byes were a pain in the ass.

So once he was mounted up, all Longarm did was ask about that foothill trail they'd mentioned earlier. Pogamogan snapped something at one of the naked boys on duty there. The kid nodded, caught Longarm's eye, and lit out running.

Longarm followed without looking back at Pogamogan and the others. The kid set a hell of a pace, and Longarm was glad he was riding after him aboard a mule. He sensed the kid was showing off a bit. A lot of desert nations initiated their young men by making them run a marathon in the heat of day, holding a mouthful of water without being allowed to swallow it as they panted through their noses. The gals were there to admire, or jeer, as the long-distance runner crossed the finish line to spit out all that water, or fail to, depending on how sincere he was about growing up to be a man of his nation.

Riding bareback at a trot was a literal ball-buster. Longarm suspected the running Indian knew that. But real men didn't get to complain of such minor discomforts unless they wanted others laughing at them. Cowboys and Indians shared some views on good clean fun.

After a while they'd made it out of that brushy canyon to a narrow trail winding southeast along a contour line of the Growler Range's cactus-covered apron. The Papago kid scampered ahead for a few furlongs, and then suddenly vanished sideways into a thick clump of jumping cholla that common sense said no naked human hide had any business in. The dramatic exit saved Longarm the trouble of trying to pronounce *skookumchuck* out loud. In any case he wasn't sure whether that meant thank you or all is well. But he said it anyway as he heeled his mule into an impolitely faster and far more comfortable lope both to warm both critters up and to make up some lost time.

You loped a mount no more than a third as much as you walked it—if you wanted it still moving under you at all by the end of your day on the trail. So Longarm reined to a walk again as the trail wound out a ways from the general slope to afford him a good hard look at the view to his southwest.

He knew the bunch he was after was somewhere down yonder on the flatter expanse between the Growlers and a sister range, looming about twenty miles away. The cactus- and chaparral-peppered flats between were covered by a spiderweb of dusty trails and dry washes, with the view complicated by the unusual weather they were having.

Drifting clouds cast almost ink-black acres of shadow across the already specked desert. They were stirred by sunbeams bright enough to hurt one's eyes and set other acres ashimmer. The only bright spot, to Longarm's way of thinking, was that while he couldn't have made out a camel caravan for certain moving yonder in any damned direction, nobody on the other side was likely to notice two bitty dots creepy-crawling along the flanks of equally distant mountains.

He felt safe lighting a smoke before he heeled his mount on to the far-away goal of Organpipe Pass. He could already picture the swell ambush site that had to go with such a name.

Folks just passing through aboard a train tended to lump organpipe cactus with the similar-looking saguaro of the Sonora Desert. But the equally proportioned organpipe grew only half the height and thickness of the forty-to-sixty-foot saguaro, and never branched the way its way bigger cousin did. It was called organpipe because it tended to grow in clusters, like the pipes of some massive gray-green church organ. So you could *hide* behind organpipe, which was tougher to manage behind the bigger but more lonesome trunks of saguaro.

"You got to *get* there before you hide ahint *shit*!" a small sardonic voice warned Longarm from the back of his skull.

Longarm had quit school early, to attend a war they were having, before he'd ever been taught any formal trigonometry. But anybody who'd ever led a distant duck with a shotgun muzzle, or learned to rope running calves from the back of a moving pony, had practiced it in his head, and the trigonometry functions he had to cope with were simple, damn each and every one of them.

Somewhere off to the southwest—he couldn't distinguish the broad main wash or narrow pony trail from his own vantage point at such far range in such tricky light— the bunch he was after had a fifteen-to-thirty-mile lead on him. To head them off at Organpipe Pass, he'd have to cover about sixty miles in the time it would take them to go thirty or forty. Writers who wrote about Sioux warriors or Mongol hordes who could ride a hundred miles a day didn't know much about riding. On a good day in cool weather a Pony Express rider would cover sixty miles in six hours, changing horses six times along the way. Riding slowed a lot when you asked the same four hooves to move that far in a full two days. The 3rd Cav still bragged about the time it had marched fifty-four miles and fought a four-hour battle within thirty-six hours during Crook's Powder River Campaign back in '76. Critters just couldn't, or wouldn't, run much more than a mile before you had to let them walk a spell. They wouldn't walk much more than an hour before you had to let them stop to rest. So unless they were some sort of wind-up toys, those incredible Mongol ponies would have to stay incredible.

Staring hard at the wide panorama to his southwest, Longarm was stuck for one corner of his big imaginary triangle. Thanks to this break in the usual August weather, nobody was kicking up a lick of trail dust whether they were moving along any damned trail or not. The cooled-off and cloudy afternoon that allowed *him* to ride by broad day after high noon offered them the same opportunity, although on riding stock that had already been pushed a fair ways.

Longarm tried to put himself under the Stetson of the

other side's trail boss. He knew they'd figured on nobody even trying to cut their trail this early, and by now they'd seen that any trail they'd been leaving had been wiped clean by that morning rain. Also, they had one woman for certain, and any number of greener riders, with them. There were more lazy bums and misfits than top hands riding the Owl-hoot Trail. So they might be inclined to laze in the cool shade of some whitebark as they let their stock graze and rest, figuring on just drifting across the border under cover of the wee small hours any old time they got around to it.

Longarm spied a clump of prickle-pear ahead, and reined in as he got out a barlow knife from the trading post stock, muttering aloud, "On the other hand, if I was in charge of that bunch I might want to push on faster, taking advantage of this break in the heat. They must have someone guiding them who knows this desert, and if there's one thing to know about this desert, it has to be that you don't get many cool days down this way in August!"

He dismounted and tethered the two mules to some handy paloverde while he went to work on that thorny but vulnerable prickle-pear with his spanking-new blade. As he lopped off and peeled pad after pad to produce two piles of what looked and likely tasted like oval servings of wa-termelon rind, he told the nearest mule, "No sense passing up a free gallon or more of extra water. I know you brutes think I'm loco, packing eighty pounds of water along through all this rain. But the desert diggers who know them better say old Waigon giveth sky water and old Tanapah taketh away. That's what they call the thunderbird and the desert sun spirit, Waigon and Tanapah. They're scared shit-less of both, with good reason."

He moved both mules closer to let them take advantage of his pulpy green treat, knowing they'd get some nutrition as well as watery sap from it.

Then little wet tree toads seemed to be hopping around the brim of Longarm's Stetson, and he looked up at the swirling clouds to declare, "Damn it, Waigon, you've rained all over us enough for one day!"

Then a thunderbolt sizzled down to turn a hundred-year-old saguaro into a steaming mist of pea-green soup, and as Longarm fought to hold the mules from bolting, he told them soothingly, "Look on the bright side. This afternoon storm might keep those others pinned down, and I don't mind getting a tad wet if you stubborn mules don't."

Chapter 5

The cavalry hated to admit it, but while horses ran faster, men and mules could cover more ground in the long run. Both trotted at about the same speed as a horse, and legged-up infantry could walk a tad faster than any riding stock. The edge dragoons or cavalry held over infantry was that a trooper who didn't have to tote his own load was in better shape to fight after he'd gotten there firstest with the mostest. That reserve burst of speed under a cavalryman's ass could move him across a field of fire faster, and sometimes rattle enemy marksmen more, than a line of charging bayonets.

When it came to forced marches across rough ground, a determined man on foot could outpace mounted rivals anywhere but dry country. The sheer weight of that vital water they were packing kept Longarm busy with the damned mules as they got ever harder to handle, hour after hour.

He walked them a lot, then rested, watered, and fed them more than he'd have ever indulged himself. He naturally changed mounts every mile or so, eighty pounds of water and thirty pounds of trail grub and such weighing less than himself and the Big Fifty. The water bags he'd filled in Pogamogan's canyon got no lighter along the trail because it would have been dumb to tap either, with rainwater running in silvery trickles or muddy brooklets down the mountain slope and across the very trail they were following.

Short spells of rain were interspersed with longer intervals of afternoon sunlight that would have baked things hotter, once they'd dried some, if more shimmering veils of torrential rain hadn't swept through every hour or less from the south. A man down to his last chips played the cards he held as best he could. So Longarm cussed and kicked the brutes along the trail as they tried to tell him they were too tired to set such a determined pace. For the wild card Longarm was playing, if he held it, was the likelihood that the others were waiting out this dying tropical storm as it bled itself to death so far from its tropical spawning grounds.

He didn't have to beat them all the way to that distant pass. He only had to get ahead of them. He'd settle for a cactus-covered rise with a clear field of fire, drop Harmony Drake first, and play out the endgame as best he could, knowing he'd at least kept his federal want from getting away. He had no doubt he could drop anyone he was aiming at with a peep-sighted Big Fifty. He was still working on how you got a *second* shot off in time.

It was getting on toward sundown when Longarm spied smoke rising up ahead and dismounted to lead his mules afoot as he regarded the odd development with the Big Fifty cradled handy.

It didn't add up right. He'd been picturing Drake and his pals off to the right, somewhere out on those lower flats. Pogamogan had told him this hillside trail was a sort of Papago secret. It was possible strangers to these part, tired of splashing through mud, might work their way to higher ground and stumble over a drier trail headed the same way they wanted to ride, but would outlaws on the run build such a smoky fire in broad day?

He murmured to the nearest mule, ''That fancy gal they

have tagging along has a way of getting menfolk to mind her and she may not be used to wet socks. Any fire you built with anything out here today would burn damp and smoky.''

They moved along until a stray eddy of air carried the smell of wood smoke and frijoles to him through the damp chaparral. It hardly seemed likely a bunch of Anglo outlaws would be having Mexican frijoles for supper. Lots of regular Americans liked chili con carne, hot tamales, and such, but frijoles were a sort of tasteless variety of mushy brown beans you had to be raised on, the way Scotchmen were fed oatmeal early on, before you'd ever bother to eat them on purpose.

Feeling a tad better, but still cautious about someone cooking a pot of Mexican beans in the middle of nowhere, Longarm tethered the two mules to some trailside whitebark and eased forward alone, allowing the muzzle of the Big Fifty to lead the way as the trail wound through the hillside scrub.

He was scouting fair enough, he thought, until some sneaky son of a bitch rose from a clump of pear he'd just passed to call out in a jovial tone, *"Buentardes, gringo. A 'onde va?"*

Longarm managed a slow turn and a sheepish smile in spite of that first impulse to leap out of his own skin. The Spanish-speaking gent with a sawed-off ten-gauge casually trained in Longarm's general direction was wearing the straw hat and white cotton outfit of a humble Mexican or gussied-up Yaqui. His dark moon face could be read either way.

It was an old trick, but tricks got old by working, so Longarm tried to sound sort of stupid as he called back, ''Me no savvy Spanny-Hole, Seen Yore. Can't you talk American, seeing we're both north of the border?''

It worked. The shotgun-wielding stranger made a dreadful remark about Longarm's mother in Spanish, but tried to sound as if butter wouldn't melt in his mouth when he re plied, "Of course I speak Anglo. I ride for El Rancho Rocking T to our north and we are out for to hunt strays, eh?"

As if to explain the big fibber's use of the plural another voice called out at some distance, *"Alo, Juan Pablo. Quien es?"*

The one confronting Longarm called back in the same lingo, *"Hemos uno pendejo con dos mulas. Comprende que queremos?"*

When the other called back in a jolly way, *"Claro, no se preocupe,"* Longarm sensed he was in trouble. When the one facing him tried not to sound worried while he casually shouted, *"Cuidado, el tiene un fusil,"* Longarm knew for certain, and simply swung the muzzle of his Big Fifty up to blast the one he could see and crab to one side and flatten down in some *creosota* while the Mexican he'd shot tried to bring down the sun with a dead finger on the trigger of his scattergun.

It felt like a million years, and might have taken as long as five seconds, for Longarm to lever down the sliding block and jam another round in the smoking chamber of the Big Fifty as he lay on his side in what smelled like a crushed drugstore, expecting to see that other Mexican looming over him with a more lethal weapon.

Then he'd reloaded, and better yet, the sounds of crashing brush were headed away instead of toward him. So he rolled up on one knee as, sure enough, a Mexican dressed the same but wearing a six-gun instead of a shotgun was breaking cover aboard a palomino barb to ride down the slope at full gallop, as if he had better places to go.

He was already out of range, had Longarm been following him with the sights of his regular saddle gun. But when he let fly with that Big Fifty, the barb found itself running under an empty saddle. So it naturally stopped a furlong down and turned to gaze back up the slope in equine confusion.

First things coming first, Longarm reloaded as he moved up to the first one he'd downed, muttering, "When you say you're covering an asshole with a couple of mules, you'd best make sure he don't savvy *Spanish*, speaking of *pendejos, pendejo.*"

The Mexican sprawled by the discharged ten-gauge was too dead to reply. The hole in his white shirtfront was only half an inch across. Most of that blood running down the slope from where he lay had to be oozing out the fist-sized exit wound.

The two of them had just proven how useful a sawed-off shotgun was in a fight at medium range in wide-open country. So Longarm saw no reason to bother with the dead man's gun as he turned to see how the other one might be doing.

Longarm knew he'd dropped the spooked rider about a quarter mile down from the trail. He lay somewhere in the smoke-blue or olive tangle of waist-high scrub and scattered tree-cactus. That pony was already working its way back to the tethered riding stock along the trail, about as fast as a kid drifting in for supper after playing in the sand-lot across the way.

As he followed the muzzle of his lethal but limited weapon on foot, Longarm muttered, as if his fallen foeman could hear him, "You don't call out that you know just what to do as you're creeping up behind a simple Americano, *amigo mio*. But in all fairness, it was your pal's warning I was packing a gun that made your full intent unmistakable. So where did I hit you and where are you at?"

He hadn't really expected anyone to answer. So it came as quite a surprise when a bare-headed man in a bloody cotton shirt suddenly rose waist-high in the chaparral, about fifty yards away, to brandish a thumb-buster Schofield .45-28 and scream, *"Te voy a mandar pa'l carajo!"*

Longarm called back, *"No hagas fregadas!* I have the drop on you at this range!"

But the badly wounded and doubtless confounded Mexican fired a wild and hopeless pistol round in Longarm's general direction, and since he had more rounds where that one had come from, Longarm nailed him dead center with a second buffalo round that picked him off his feet and tossed him out of sight in the shrubbery again.

Longarm still reloaded as he moved in. When you were packing a single-shot rifle, you didn't assume a man who'd only been hit twice with buffalo-droppers was fixing to just lie there.

But when Longarm found his victim, sprawled across another ant pile and already covered with the bitty red devils, he could only say in a not unkind voice, "At least I had the courtesy to kill you first. I was about to say I'd like to go through your pockets. But seeing you ain't got any pockets in those glorified pajamas, I'd best settle for that rusty six-gun over yonder. I hope you have extra ammo in your saddlebags."

He turned to retrace his steps, picking up the Schofield along the way. A bit of added motion joined his own long shadow as it proceeded him. So he glanced over his left shoulder to see that, sure enough, a flock of those brown hawks and at least two buzzards were taking an interest in proceedings from where they circled on a rising column of afternoon warming. He knew it was the tethered stock and his own moving form that kept them pinned to the sky. He grimaced, told them to just hold the thought a spell, and trudged on up to the earlier scene of carnage.

The first Mexican he'd gunned had pockets in his more substantial white pants. But the fistful of gold and silver coins didn't say a thing that could have been used against the dead cuss in court. Everybody knew an honest *vaquero* riding for some ranch in the middle of nowhere got paid off in U.S. silver dollars and Mexican double eagles worth about twenty of the same.

Longarm put the sixty-odd dollars worth of specie in his own pants pocket, feeling better about the money he'd lost in Growler Wash the other night.

There were four rounds left in the wheel of the single-action army pistol, cheaper than the already cheap but more popular Colt '73 Improved Model, or Peacemaker. The dead Mexican had been packing it cheap in his waistband. Longarm had no choice but to stick it in his own the same way. He was glad it was single-action as he felt its steel barrel chill his gut. Dreadful accidents had resulted from hasty grabs at a double-action six-gun stuffed down the front of a man's pants. A fast draw was out of the question, of course, but at least he'd be set for taking on more than one enemy at a time, and he figured he had at least five men and a mighty mean woman to deal with before he could say for certain who'd won.

He found that palomino barb nuzzled up with a sorrel mare, tied to some more paloverde near that hasty campfire they'd baited him with when they'd spotted him first in the distance. The fire had gone out under the tin can of water and frijoles. He'd already noted frijoles were an acquired taste, and he knew those birds up yonder were more hungry right now. So he gathered the two ponies and his mules in one bunch and led them on foot a decorous distance away, muttering, "Those obvious outlaws would have left *this* child for the buzzards, and we're pressed for time in any case. So why don't I peel you all some pear and go through some saddlebags as we all get to know one another a tad better?"

The riding stock didn't argue. The two Mexican ponies were as used to the taste of skinned-out cactus as the Papago mules. The only clue to anyone's identity was a crumpled reward poster, in Spanish, saying that the governor of Sonora would pay a thousand pesos for the head of one

Juan Pablo Ebanista, wanted for everything *including* poor church attendance. There was nothing on the other wayward youth.

Longarm discarded the dirty spare duds, filthy bedrolls, and dried grub the two of them had been packing. The same wet spell that had cleaned both exposed tree-dally saddles had spoiled their jerked beef, cornmeal, and beans.

He had no use for their canteens at the moment, but left them in place just in case, once he'd rinsed them out and refilled the four of them from a sandy puddle of standing rainwater by the trail. For the late afternoon sky was rapidly clearing, with the low western sun outlining the remaining clouds in bright gold, and they'd never named these parts a desert because it rained with any regularity.

Longarm found and treasured half a box of .45-28 Army Shorts for the poorly kept Schofield tucked in his pants. The army issued, and lost, a lot of underpowered but heavy slugs with the same reasoning it issued easy-to-maintain but slow-firing small arms. Recruiting many an immigrant greenhorn into its low-paid ranks, the army didn't want any kid who'd never handled a gun before blazing away all his ammunition at once, or flinching from recoil too much to aim the one shot at a time they wanted from him. So they'd turned down the original 40-grain charges offered by more than one bemused gunmaker in favor of the shorter and more gently kicking army rounds.

The ubiquitous Schofield was an army ordinance design rather than a brand. Although Smith & Wesson made the most of the break-front notions of Major George—not General John—Schofield. Meant to be packed as only a backup to a trooper's rifle or carbine, the rugged but far from ideal six-gun might hit an aimed-at target fifty yards away. But the small kick sacrificed any killing power the Schofield had past, say, a hundred yards.

All five of those outlaws he was trailing, and likely that mean gal, packed .45 or .44-40 side arms that could kill, with any luck, from five times as far away. The only edge Longarm had was the Big Fifty, if they weren't expecting him to aim anything that awesome their way. Gunfighters expecting regular gunfighting might expose themselves at what they considered the safe distance of five hundred yards, a dead-easy bull's-eye with a Big Fifty.

But like the old gospel song said, they'd know more about that farther along. So once he had his superabundance of riding stock watered and fed on cactus pulp, and seeing he knew the mules far better, Longarm shifted his water bags but no trail supplies to the mule he'd been riding, tethered the four of them along one of the Mexican's rawhide riatas, and mounted that palomino barb to get acquainted as he got them all on up the trail.

By sundown he'd ridden all four brutes, and knew the sorrel mare and the taller of the two mules were less trouble. The smaller mule had been fighting the lead for some time. The palomino barb seemed to feel much the same way as its previous owner about riders who spoke to it in English. Longarm could have managed any two of the four if he'd had to. But he didn't have to, and the constant argument was slowing them all a bit. So when he stopped for another trail break while the sun set glorious in a fluffy bed of red and gold, Longarm put the most comfortable of the two Mexican saddles on the more willing mule, tossed the other in a circle of greasewood down the slope, and cut a length of riata to loosely tether the stubborn mule and surly palomino together as he gently explained to the pony, "I don't like you either. But it would be cruel to leave you to find your own way out here, with the air already commencing to smell dry again. So stick with this mule and you'll both wind up back in that Papago camp, where you'd better learn to control your damned temper, hear?"

The pony lashed out with a hind hoof as Longarm hit the mule it was with across the rump. Then they were both escaping from him down the trail with snorts of equine mischief. Longarm had to laugh too. Then he mounted the more reasonable mule, gently jerked the lead he'd tied to the sorrel's bridle, and led off to the southeast at a ball-busting but mile-eating trot.

Getting to stand in the tapped stirrups of that easy-riding Mexican saddle seemed a treat at any pace after all that bareback riding. The saddle had been invented with that in mind. The Mexican-made Moorish ancestor of the American stock saddle, despite its cantle and swells of exposed cottonwood, was if anything more chairlike. For while Anglo cowhands preferred to fall clear of a cartwheeling pony when things went wrong, the Mexican *vaquero* was inclined to be more fatalistic about the possible future, and preferred his ass comfortable in the here and now. So the saddle Longarm had salvaged for his trotting mule cradled the bigger frame of an Anglo rider as if the bare wood had been molded to his thighs and pelvis like clay. He'd already made a mental note not to risk a downhill lope in the dark aboard such a dangerously comfortable saddle. It hardly seemed likely either mount was likely to fall under him along the sandy trail, even as it got tougher to make out. He knew all riding stock saw better than he did in the dark. The one good thing to be said for your mount being dumber than another human, or even a dog, was that you could count on it to just stop when it couldn't tell what was in front of it. You had to be smart enough to *care* what a master thought of you before you'd take really stupid chances.

As the sky kept clearing, the stars got awesomely bright against the blackness of what was again a dried-out desert sky. You never really got to lick your eyes across the Milky Way where there were any street lights at all. But those old-timers who'd made up all the names for the stars had been desert dwellers too. So riding under the same breed of night sky, you could see what they'd been jawing about in those old astrology books. That big old Dog Star, staring down from the August sky, really did look hot-tempered and glaring when you got to stare back at it. He'd heard those Moors who'd taught the Spanish so much about roping and riding had named one star up yonder ''The Ghoul,'' ghoul being a Moorish word, because of the way it got dim and bright, mysterious and sort of spooky, next to the other stars. He couldn't make out any ghoulish stars, but that distinctly red one closer to the horizon had to be old Mars, which was said to be a world like this one, all covered with red deserts, like the Four Corners up the other side of the Gila. Nobody could say whether there might be any *folks* roaming the Martian deserts. Longarm waved a howdy in any case.

Then the moon came up, lemon yellow as it rose above the jet-black fangs of the jaggedy Growlers, to bathe everything for miles around in a ghostly glow that set coyotes to howling and things in the brush all about to skittering.

The pony had farted five times in as many recent minutes, so it seemed a good time to combine more than one concern. Longarm reined in, dismounted, and broke out the nose bags he'd packed for the two mules with occasions such as this one in mind. He put a generous but thoughtful amount of water and cracked corn in each bag, and put them on both brutes before he unsaddled them both to dry as they munched and lazed beside the trail.

Then he and the Big Fifty went up the slope a furlong to see what could be seen out yonder in the moonlight.

Many a critter was stirring, judging by the faint sounds in all directions. But the lower moonlit expanse to the southwest stared back up at him as innocent as carpet in an empty drawing room. He couldn't make out the better-known trail along the main drainage between the neighboring ranges. If those others had built a fire, they knew how to hide it in a deep wash after dark. He figured it was more likely they were on the move, wherever the hell they thought they were, right now.

He resisted the impulse to reach for a smoke, warning himself how the flare of a match could be spotted from three miles or more by a human eye adjusted to the night. He could only hope some greenhorn on the other side might not know this. There was just too much *yonder* out yonder for his own night vision to really draw a bead on anything that didn't look like brush or cactus.

He sat down, bracing his elbows on his upraised knees with the Big Fifty across his lap, as he willed his impatient body to relax and settle down a spell. He knew that neither the sorrel nor that mule were half as anxious as he was to head anyone off at any fool pass. They needed some serious rest while that solid food sank in. Riding stock farted that way when it ate too much green clover too. Any cavalryman who'd ever ridden down an Indian on a grass-fed pony could tell you it took solid grain to sustain a mount beyond a few short hours in the field.

As he lowered his head to his crossed arms, Longarm warned himself not to let himself go all the way to sleep. Then he remembered other times like this and sighed, "Aw, shit, we're only human."

So the next thing he knew he was waking up from a dumb dream with a piss hard-on, shivering and goose-fleshed under his hickory shirt, to see the moon had moved quite a ways from the last time he'd looked up at it.

He would have turned over and gone back to sleep if this had been his furnished digs in Denver. But it wasn't, so Longarm groaned himself to his feet, pissed on a patch of bare caliche, and headed back down to the trail, where he found both his equine pals had been dozing and pissing themselves.

He loaded up and mounted the sorrel to take up the slow but steady chase, knowing it all depended on how disciplined or self-indulgent the outlaws had been.

He got a little trotting and a lot of walking out of the mismatched pair he'd selected from a choice of four. He gave them a trail break once every ninety minutes or so, and forced himself to take another catnap in the wee small hours, when the cold night air woke him even sooner. Then the clear sky was pearling pale in the east, and he could see farther across the wide-open spaces he seemed to ride alone. The slopes to his left were less steep. The distant hills of sunset were now much closer. The valley between was less flat as well as more narrow. He could see how they were funneling their way to that shallow pass he'd been told about.

He knew two could play at most any game. So he dropped down off the higher trail he'd been following all night to find that, sure enough, a wider trail did wend its way southeast through the thicker desert growth where rains soaked in deeper.

But Longarm wasn't half as interested in the cactus and stickerbrush as he was in the all-too-clear hoofmarks in the rain-smoothed sand of the damned old trail. They'd already made it this far, six shod and two unshod head, adding up just right for it to be them and all wrong for him to follow.

He dismounted anyway and struck a match to make sure. The sons of bitches had a four-to-six-hour lead on him. There was no way he could catch up this side of the border, and he had direct orders to never darken the door of El Presidénte Diaz again. So how was he ever going to obey directly conflicting orders from the Denver District Court in the person of Marshal Billy Vail?

He'd been told to go fetch Harmony Drake from that Yuma jail, and he'd been warned not to cause another international incident down Mexico way. That was what they called it when you had to shoot a Mexican *rurale*.

So the gambling boys would have assured Longarm that he'd done his best but lost the game, and that it was time to get up from the table and head back to report that his man had simply gotten away from him, along with his badge and gun. That way, at least nobody could accuse him of refusing to obey a direct order, right?

Longarm rose with a sigh, walked back to the mule he was riding now, while the pony carried the pack, and morosely informed them both, "I know the two of you are tired. I am too. We still have to push on. Those sons of bitches seem bound and determined to get this child into another damned war with Mexico. But I still aim to take Harmony Drake, dead or alive!"

Chapter 6

Mules and ponies were only human, but any number could play the ambush game. So Longarm kept their unavoidable trail breaks as short as possible, and punched through Organpipe Pass after moonset and just before dawn.

There was nobody trying to hold the pass, which was more of a notch in the higher tableland to the south than a gap between real ridges. There was nobody guarding the border, wherever it was, when Longarm must have crossed it before noon. For the fresh sign on the trail he was following with a grim smile and a Big Fifty wound through what was a natural hell to patrol—or a paradise for cactus, large and small.

Something about the soil or the way clouds swept across that higher patch of desert had resulted in a tangled mess of organpipe, lots of saguaro, and way too much cholla, with a peculiar Mexican relation of saguaro that grew prone across the ground, like a green spiny python, to tangle its upright cousins in thorny logjams. You had to pick your way carefully through such tedious desert patches. He could see the rascals he was trailing had. The occasional horse apple he spotted in the now-dry dust looked dusty and fly-blown enough to give them a good twelve-hour lead on him, blast Rosalinda and his own weak nature.

He had to give in to the natural needs of his equine pals as the sun glared down on their weary hides from the dead center of that blue dome. There was no hint of breeze from either side of the cactus-lined trail, and the mule he was leading kept fighting the line like a fish that just didn't want to be hauled any higher and drier.

Longarm reined in and dismounted, muttering, "When you're right you're right. It's fixing to get way hotter before it cools a tad, and Drake's gang have likely holed up for *la siesta* by now down the trail a piece."

He led his nearly spent stock between two clumps of organpipe and over one of those reclining whatevers toward a grove of wicked cholla. The mule had likely stuck its muzzle on cholla before, and tried to tell this to Longarm.

The fortunately strong-wristed deputy jerked the line the other way and said, "I know what I'm doing, mule. I know cholla looks and acts like the Devil's own crab-apple tree. But the really nasty thorns all sprout from the pads on the ends of those corky limbs, and the trunks holding all that mischief off the ground don't have any thorns at all."

Holding both leads in his left hand with the sling of the Big Fifty, Longarm proceeded to carefully but quickly lop away the hellish fuzzy cholla pads that needed plenty of sunlight to go with the tree-like roots of its cork-barked trunk. Once he'd cleared a less dangerous overhang, he led first the pony and then the mule through, holding their heads low to clear the vicious thorns of the archway.

Inside the ancient cholla grove, they found it a shady if low-ceilinged bower, with clean caliche between the trunks a yard or more apart. The dense shade of closely packed cactus pads had killed anything else that had ever sprouted there, and the thrifty desert critters had carried every dry scrap away as grub or bedding.

Longarm tethered both brutes with their heads low and put extra water in their nose bags, along with a double ration of cracked corn. He knew the parched grain would go on swelling after the stock had downed it. But you seldom bloated a critter if you let it have its fill of water before it ate and you didn't let it eat too much.

He unloaded them and set packs and saddle well clear, with the Mexican saddle upside down and its blanket shaken out flat on the dry caliche. Then he inspected all eight hooves for splits or pebbles, unpacked his tarp and one thin flannel blanket, stripped to the buff, wiped himself head to toe with a damp rag, and treated himself to all the flat warm rubber-scented water he felt like drinking before he positioned the Big Fifty and Schofield on his spread-to-dry duds and flopped flat atop the flannel, the shade cool on his naked hide, as he numbly wondered how he'd managed to get so sleepyheaded all of a sudden.

Then he was in the Denver Public Library, looking for an Atlas so he could look up Puerto Peñasco and see how far those rascals had to ride for that blamed steamboat to Far Cathay, only he'd just noticed he was naked as a jay.

Nobody else seemed to notice as he sat down at a reading table to hide his uncalled-for erection. But then the librarian came over to tell him he wasn't allowed to smoke. So he snubbed out a cheroot he hadn't notice he was smoking and explained, "I figure they have at least one experienced border-jumper with them, ma'am. So they'll want to avoid that border town of Sonoyta and the *rurales* stationed there. I'm still trying to decide whether they'd be better off making their crossing after dark, when *los rurales* can't see as far but expect folks to cross, or—"

"Never mind all that, Deputy Long," the librarian said. "How do you like the way my husband and I have been doing so far, and are you out to avoid another international incident for us or not?"

Longarm hadn't noticed till then that he was talking to Miss Lemonade Lucy Hayes, the President's handsome but sort of stuffy wife. She'd had her clothes on the time she'd

erved him orange punch instead of her notorious lemonade
t the White House in Washington Town. Now he tried not
o notice her middle-aged but not unattractive naked torso
s he soberly replied, "Your man and me have about
leaned up the Indian Ring left over from the Grant Ad-
ninistration, and I've always been in favor of sound money
nd the end of Reconstruction, ma'am. I ain't working on
hat lost, strayed, or stolen gift from Queen Victoria right
ow. I'm chasing plain old outlaws across the Mexican bor-
ler. I know they don't want me to do that any more. But
had orders to deliver the rascal to the Denver District
Court too, so . . ."

"Why don't we go back amongst the stacks and make
nad Gypsy love?" the First Lady suggested, coyly adding,
'I don't hold with drinking hard liquor, but I've always
iked *other* things hard."

Longarm gulped and politely replied, "I ain't sure we
ught to, uh, ma'am. If screwing the President's wife ain't
igh treason, it has to qualify as disrespect to a superior."

"Who says so? Who? Who? Who?" demanded Lem-
nade Lucy in a desperate tone. Then Longarm opened his
leep-gummed eyes and, still hearing the same repeated
question, propped himself up on one elbow to see that a
lock of gnatcatchers were mobbing an elf owl, perched on
nearby cholla branch. He didn't see why. Owls holed up
luring the hours the fluttery gnatcatchers were using the
ky. But he thanked them all in any case, saying, "I might
ave had a mighty disrespectful wet dream, or worse yet,
verslept."

The elf owl flew away with its smaller tormentors tag-
;ing after it all atwitter. It was odd how the human voice
:ould spook some critters more than a thrown boot. He'd
noticed in the past you could get pack rats to quit stirring
bout at night by just asking them, in a polite tone, to quit.

One of those bastards riding with Harmony Drake had
_ongarm's watch. But the way the sunbeams slanted

through the cholla pads above him said it was after three in the afternoon by now.

Longarm dragged his naked form erect in the decidedly warm shade, and moved over to the tethered riding stock muttering, "Howdy. Are you two as thirsty as I am right now?"

They were, he saw, when he removed their empty nose bags to see they'd been licking at the bare bottoms of the bucket-like canvas containers. He filled them partway with tepid water from the handy rubberized bags, and put them back in place before he helped himself to some of the mighty uninteresting liquid.

The canyon springwater had tasted tangy when he'd filled the bags back at Pogamogan's camp. This afternoon it tasted as if it had been boiled in an old rubber boot, which it had in a way. But looking on the bright side, it was easier to husband the water your body just had to replace in this dry heat. It would have been a total bitch to pack all the cold beer a man would be tempted to put away on days like this.

His riding stock made short work of their first helping. He poured more for them, saying, "Take it easy and don't drown yourselves on your feet. I saw a greenhorn do that to an army mule one time. He filled the nose bag higher than the poor brute's nostrils, and took all that kicking and snorting for high spirits."

Receiving no answer, Longarm went back to his bedding and hauled on his duds and boots, with some reluctance. He had felt hot enough naked in the shade.

He ate a can of pork and beans from the trading post and rinsed it down with tomato preserves. Then he lit a smoke and watched three zebra-tail lizards play tag around a nearby cholla trunk. It was ten times hotter than it should have been, but at least twenty degrees cooler than it had been around high noon. Lizards and other cold-blooded desert critters got in most of their fun in the few hours be

68

tween too hot and too cold in these parts.

He hated to even think about it, but since he didn't know whether those other border jumpers planned an early or late crossing, he had to go with as early a crossing as practical.

That meant soon, damn it. *Los rurales* would just be breaking their own siestas about now. They'd tank up on coffee and saddle up for an evening patrol as the shadows lengthened. Anyone slipping across the line about *now* would likely make it without meeting up with *los rurales*. Anyone waiting for the cool shade of evening and the cloak of darkness would be risking a moonlit tryst with old desert hands who knew how to sit a pony silent and listen to the night noises all about.

Longarm sighed, gripped the cheroot between bared teeth, and rolled up the bedding. The mule and pony bared their teeth a bit too as they grasped his full intent to load them back up and lead them back out into that glaring sunlight.

He did it anyway, and all three had been right about it feeling as if they'd stepped through an oven door. The sun was far lower in the west, but it felt as if you were breathing alkali dust through cobwebs.

Longarm led the way afoot as far as the trail. Then, seeing those same hoofprints that had preceded him south at some damned time in the past, he mounted the mule to lead the sorrel mare and their depleted water supply at a trot.

He had at least one member of the gang pictured as an hombre who knew these parts. Longarm didn't need a map to tell him this trail had to lead to the village of Sonoyta. Trails generally led somewhere, and Sonoyta was the only border town for miles to the east or west.

The question was why he or the outlaws he was trailing would want to go there. Strangers riding into small desert towns always drew a good deal of attention. Anglo riders in a Mexican border town were apt to draw more than their fair share from the local *rurales*.

There was the unpleasant possibility that an owlhoot rider in the habit of crossing the border in these parts might have come to some sort of understanding with the local *rurale* captain. A lot of Longarm's own problems with Mexico's answer to the Texas Rangers sprang from their almost cheerful demands for bribes, whether you'd done anything or not.

Then, just as he was starting to really worry about some son of a bitch with his badge and gun and a *rurale* company as well, Longarm saw the hoofprints he'd been following veer off to the east through a patch of stirrup-deep *creosota*.

He smiled wolfishly and told his mount, "The odds ain't as bad as we feared. *Los rurales* are likely to shoot all of us for our boots except Goldmine Gloria. They won't shoot *her* before they've all had their turn with her. I wonder why we're riding east. I'd have thought it would be shorter to that seaport sixty miles or so away if we swung around Sonoyta to the *west*."

Neither critter seemed to want to trot in either direction. So Longarm dismounted to lead on foot at a walk as he scouted for sign in the greened-up desert.

That philosopher who'd first remarked on what a difference a day could make had likely ridden the Sonora Desert in his time. Cactus flowered in the spring, dry or wet, as if remembering they'd once been rosier. But other stuff with no way to store as much water paid more attention to the weather than the calendar. So fairy dusters were already sprouting feathery little leaves, and the scattered clumps of paloverde, which was usually a sort of gigantic witch's broom of bare green sticks, were starting to bud like pussy willow. *Tomatillo* and *jobjola* brush that had looked dead and dried out before that rain were suddenly green and perky as if they'd been growing in a park back East. Staring down at the crust of caliche for hoofprints, Longarm made out microscopic flowers he'd have otherwise missed. They were mostly yellow, but came in all colors, as if meant to go in some little gal's doll house in a teeny-tiny vase.

The bunch he was trailing had spread some to ride through the paloverde and cactus clumps. So Longarm concentrated on just one set of prints, left by a pony who'd thrown its near rear shoe as its rider set as direct a course as possible almost due east.

An hour off the trail Longarm had to lead around the flyblown remains of a roadrunner someone had blasted almost in two, likely with a pistol shot.

"Miserable bastards," Longarm muttered as he skirted the column of flies above the pathetic ruins of a recently lively clown-bird. It wasn't hard to kill roadrunners. They got their name from their habit of scampering along with desert travelers, likely to catch the sneakier critters flushed by hooves or wagon wheels. No Indian would dream of harming such a friendly critter with such tasteless stringy meat. Mexicans admired them because they cleared the roads of scorpions, rattlesnakes, and such. But there was a variety of Anglo asshole that simply couldn't resist taking potshots at road signs, saguaros, songbirds, or anything else that wasn't likely to shoot back.

"They passed this way by daylight," Longarm assured the mule as they hurried on. He had no call to tell a Papago mule that roadrunners patrolled for snakes, lizards, and bugs early in the morning or late in the afternoon. The poor dead bird was too flyblown for death within the past few hours. It wouldn't have come out of the shade to get shot by a prickhead it was only funning with during the siesta hours just past. Longarm decided the outlaws were eight or ten hours ahead of him. Even less, if they'd holed up out ahead for their own siesta.

He knew he had that edge if anyone was lying in wait out ahead. He didn't see why anyone would be, but they'd have the late sun in their eyes while he'd be aiming at a well-lit target. Old U. S. Grant had told his boys they'd have the sunrise at their backs as they advanced at Cold

Harbor. Old U. S. Grant had gotten one hell of a heap of his boys killed at Cold Harbor, come to study on it. But it might have been worse had the sun been shining the other way.

He almost fell over the edge of the dry wash winding south to north through the cactus and stickerbush. You had to be right on top of it to know it was there. Once you did, the brushy bottom was so shaded that Miss Cleopatra could have been performing a snake dance in those inky shadows for all he could tell from up where *he* was.

It got much easier to see as soon as he and his riding stock had worked down a crumbling wall to the sandy bottom. Flood waters had scoured the center of the wash clean, save for the neatly defined hoofprints left by the bunch he'd been trailing. He wasn't at all surprised to see they were all headed south, towards what had to be a nearby border now.

"Slick," Longarm reluctantly grunted as he paused to change the Mexican saddle back to the sorrel mare for a spell. He watered both brutes again, forked himself into that hardwood saddle, and followed the spoor of the fugitives up the wash.

It was running north out of higher desert because the original peace treaty had set the border along the Gila River to the north. That had left things awkward for both countries before the Gadsden Purchase had drawn a new imaginary line, designed to leave the natural watershed of the east-west Gila to Uncle Sam and the Southern Pacific Railroad. But in point of fact, Mexico had wound up with the headwaters of many a desert stream running downhill to the north. It hadn't been raining when they'd surveyed the Gadsden Purchase.

So this wandering wash he was following likely began as a dried-out mud puddle somewhere south of the border, but with any luck, it didn't matter to Mexico anyway.

Longarm patted the sorrel's neck and muttered, "Five

will get you ten those *banditos* rode you and your palomino pal down this very wash the other way before we had all that rain.''

He glanced back to see their own hoofprints were adding a mighty clear picture to the ones they were following. *Los rurales* were no damned good, but they were skilled man-hunters, and anyone could see a heap of likely prosperous Yanqui riders had come up this same fool wash without bothering anyone at the regular crossing.

He hummed a few bars of ''Farther Along'' as he rode on after the others, hoping their guide had some clear plan in mind.

It was almost as pleasant as a hot Denver day in July down here in the shadows cast by the high banks and thicker brush. No members of the cactus tribe could survive with their shallower roots spread in sand that got scoured about once a year, of course. But the water that lay deeper in the drying sand encouraged mesquite, ironwood, and hackberry, all of it greened out again as if it thought this was May, for Pete's sake, and the critters that usually holed up in the summer daylight of the desert were acting frisky all about, which was sort of distracting, but meant nobody was sitting in ambush around the next bend, at least.

Cicadas buzzed, white-wings cooed, and woodpeckers hammered in the olive greenery to either side as big blue-gray dragonflies chased red-eyed cactus flies about like kids playing tag after school. Now and again a ground squirrel cussed him, and once he flushed a comical desert jackrabbit with impossible ears and a zigzag way of running that made Longarm suspect some of those buzzards high above. He knew one breed of desert hawk grew black feathers and held its wings out the same way as a harmless buzzard until it saw fresh meat on the move down below. This highly evolved desert held lots of such grim surprises for the un-wary.

Longarm wasn't all that surprised when they cut through

some brush to see the sand ahead all trampled and strewn with dried scraps and the shit of man and beast. The remains of more than one cookfire told Longarm this was where the border-patrolling *rurales* paused to brew some coffee out of sight of prying eyes. *Los rurales* were out to jump border raiders and truculent Indians, not vice versa.

You couldn't make out any particular set of tracks across the abused stretch of wash. That meant a Mexican detachment, a *big* Mexican detachment, had been through here since the last rain. It was as likely a *federale* or army column as the usual *rurale* patrol. Longarm hurried on lest the usual evening patrol catch him admiring all the scattered sign down here.

He caught up with the sign of Harmony Drake's bunch on the cleaner sand upstream. He followed it because he had to. But he still wondered what in blue blazes was supposed to prevent the next *rurale* patrol from Sonoyta from cutting and following such a blatant trail.

Then, less than an hour on, he saw how the hoofprints he'd been following led up the now-much-lower western wall of the wash. So he reined in, swapped saddles and packs again, and rode the mule up into the blazing rays of the the setting sun.

It felt as if he was riding into an open fireplace, as late in the day as it was. He had to stare down to one side to make out the hoofprints the others had left in the caliche, etched almost black against salmon pink by the low sun.

They led him, just around sundown, back to that same desert trail, or one just like it, leading south *from* Sonoyta instead of *towards* such a nosy border town. Better yet, there were lots of other hoofprints headed both ways. It figured to be the main post road from the border town to the coast town of Puerto Peñasco.

Longarm muttered, "*Mighty* slick!" as he reined south to follow, not the sign he could no longer read, but the road that had to lead much the same way. It was not only possible but likely the fugitives would part company with this well-beaten track before it led them past curious eyes on the main streets of Puerto Peñasco. But there was no better place to catch a steamboat bound for the far horizon than the only seaport for many a dreary mile. The desert came right down to the sea, from the Colorado-Gila delta to the Rio Sonora to the distant south, and they were as good as caught if they tarried all that long in any part of Mexico. For *los rurales* could read, and there was a lot of bounty money posted for Harmony Drake.

As he rode at a trot in the gathering dusk, Longarm tried not to think about the Mexican reward posters offering handsome bounties on El Brazo Largo, *muerto o vivo*.

Which translated fairly tightly as "Longarm, dead or alive."

Chapter 7

A couple of dark hours down the road, Longarm topped a rise to see lamplight ahead. A *lot* of lamplight ahead. Someone had lit up the front of a wayside 'dobe structure as if they'd been expecting company.

Longarm wasn't sure of his own reception. So he rode the sorrel and led the mule off to one side through the cactus and brush until he figured he'd be out of range of all that lamplight as he circled in for a look-see.

It only took a few minutes. Longarm tethered his stock and moved in afoot with the Big Fifty at port. Standing close to a far taller clump of organpipe, he could make out an anxious-looking older Mexican in the open doorway across the road. Sun-faded blue lettering across the buff adobe above the door and windows proclaimed the place to be a *fonda por coches* or stagecoach stop. Longarm hadn't known there was a coach line from Sonyata down to that steamboat line on the Sea of Cortez, but it made sense.

He decided it made more than sense as he slipped back to where he'd tethered his now sincerely jaded riding stock. The *fondero* in that doorway was obviously expecting a night coach to Puerto Peñasco. His relay *fonda* was about ten or twelve miles south of the border. A stagecoach was called a stagecoach because it changed team in stages, every hour or so, which was about as far as one could drive a team at a steady trot. So even though it seemed to be running late, the Mexican stage from Sonoyta was likely to overtake anyone just riding along on one weary mount, or hell, beat the fugitives into Sonoyta with time to spare and pocket jingle to buy some serious side arms and get set to greet their arrival from a chosen vantage point!

Longarm knew the fleeing felons hadn't jumped the border near a *rurale* post to buy passage south aboard a faster stagecoach. He had no desire to alarm the already worried Mexican more than he had to either. So he worked his way back to the road and rode in at a walk, singing "La Paloma" off key to let everyone know he wasn't sneaking up on them.

The older Mexican in white cotton, but with boots befitting his social station, stepped out into the road as Longarm approached. As Longarm rode into the lamplight, the *fondero* indicated he'd noticed Longarm's accent by calling out, *"Buenoches, Señor.* Have you see anything of the mail coach from Sonoyta? Was supposed to be here by this time, and is not good for to leave the relay team harnessed so long before they have a load for to pull, eh?"

Longarm reined in as he replied, "I haven't seen anyone on this road south of the border but myself." Which was the simple truth, as soon as you studied on it.

Getting no argument about that, he continued. "I was hoping I might still be able to board that night coach. I can't understand it, but this stock I've only ridden a short way seems about to founder under me and I have a steamboat to meet in Puerto Peñasco!"

The *fondero* said, "We can board your stock and give you a faster ride, if that *fregado* coach ever *gets* here. Come inside for to drink with me in a more civilized position. I will have my *muchachos* take care of your jaded riding stock and we shall see what we shall see."

Longarm allowed that was the best offer he'd had since sundown, and the two of them were soon seated at one of the blue wooden tables inside, being served *pulque* in earthenware mugs by a pleasantly plump cantina gal who liked to feel cool above the nipples, judging from the way she wore her pleated cotton blouse.

Pulque tasted better when a man was really dry, which might have been why the slightly slimy home brew was more popular south of the border. Longarm was thirsty enough to have enjoyed his own spit if he'd had more to spare. So he meant it when he told them both it was really swell *pulque*.

The older *fondero* rattled off some orders in rapid-fire Spanish to the gal, who dimpled at Longarm and headed back to see that the other help carried them out. Longarm kept his face blank, lest they savvy how well he savvied their lingo. So far, nobody seemed to plotting against him or his four-footed traveling companions.

The older man opined there might not be any coach at all coming down the road that night. He explained how Los Yanquis Negros had brushed with Victorio at a place called Los Manantiales de Culebra de Cascabel and chased him across the border into Chihuahua.

Longarm frowned thoughtfully and mused half to himself, "If Black Yankees signifies the 10th Cav down from Fort Sill, which it ought to, and if they just chased four hundred Bronco Apache across the Tex-Mex border into Chihuahua from a part of the states *we're* more likely to call Rattlesnake Springs, I'm stuck. How would Indian fighting so far to the east have any bearing on whether you'd be expecting a night coach to Pueto Peñasco or not?"

The *fondero* explained, "Our own army garrison here in Sonora is on the way to join other *federales* in Chihuahua. You were so right when you said that *diablo grosero* has many riders following him!"

Longarm finished his *pulque* and, not wanting more, got

out two cheroots as he quietly repeated his observation that any number of Apache on the far side of the Sierra Madres were hardly likely to stop any stagecoaches over this way.

The *fondero* again explained. ''Apache are not the problem. *Banditos* are the problem. Since all this trouble to the east has drawn so many of our soldiers and mounted police away, the *segunderos de la calle* who seldom show their dirty faces have grown bolder. There has been much stealing of cows, and even horses, this summer. They say that the big gang led by El Gato Notorio has been seen on our side of the Sierra Madre!''

Longarm lit the older man's smoke for him as he said without too much thought that he'd heard El Gato was more a rebel than a bandit.

He regretted saying it when the older man rose to his feet with a remark about late coaches and stomped out the back way to see how his boys were doing with the stock. It was easy to forget how divided opinion could be about El Presidénte Porfirio Diaz down this way. The smooth-talking but murderous *mestizo* had stolen the liberation movement of Juarez according to some, while others opined that the one-time top general of the late Benito Juarez had now given Mexico the law, order, and stable government it needed.

That was what they called a government that treated most of its citizens like riding stock: a stable government. Taxes got collected, the mail got delivered, and you could usually count on making rail and steamboat connections, wherever that fool stagecoach *was* this evening.

El Presidénte and his Wall Street pals liked to say Mexico was now a smoothly running land of contented citizens. *Los rurales* shot citizens who wouldn't say they *were* contented. They'd have hardly hired a sworn enemy of the state for this mail coach line either.

But the fat was in the fire. So when that plump serving wench came in through another door to ask if he'd like something to eat, he pasted a smile across his face and replied, "I'm not sure I'll have the time, Señorita. I have to beat that steamboat to Puerto Peñasco whether the coach is running or not tonight."

She insisted, "I shall serve you some *huevos fritos con jamon* in no time at all. You will be able to meet that *barco costanero* with the time to spare if you have for to walk. Is only one a week either way. Your Yanqui friends from Yuma will not reach Puerto Peñasco for at least four days, *comprende*?"

He digested that and asked, "How soon might the next northbound arrive with, say, my *Mexican* friends?"

She shrugged her bare shoulders and replied, "The day after *mañana,* I think. Is the same slow but steady *vapor,* puffing north and south, south and north, in a most tedious manner on a calm but sultry sea. You say you have friends in the *south* of my country, Señor?"

He said he'd sure like those ham and eggs now. So she went out back to fry them, or get somebody else to do so. The place seemed to be crawling with unseen kids, or maybe brownies, judging from the muffled elfin giggles.

The old *fondero* came back in, still smoking what was left of that cheroot. He said he'd put away the sorrel and mule. He also said he'd left Longarm's saddle and baggage in the tack room next to the stable. Then he said he'd told his help to put the coach team they'd harnessed back in their damned stalls as well, seeing that coach was so late now, it would have to finish its run by broad day—in August, *Jesus, Maria y Jose!*

Longarm said he was waiting for a late snack, and asked about a coach ticket to go with it.

The grumpy old cuss said to settle with the *cochero* about his passage and the accommodations that went with it, when and if the triple-thumbed *pendejo* ever showed up with that *chingado* coach.

Longarm followed his drift. Out-of-the-way layouts such

as this one were less attractive to road agents if they let the coach crew deal with most of the cash on hand.

The older man accepted another cheroot. But when the cantina gal returned with Longarm's ham and eggs, the *fondero* allowed it was past his own bedtime and rose to leave.

Longarm said, "Hold on. If I can't catch a coach out of here, how do you feel about swapping me two fresh mules for the mule and swell pony I rode in on?"

The *fondero* shook his head and replied, "Is not for me to decide such matters for *la compañia,* as fine as the sorrel seems. I mean no disrespect, but did you not say they began to give out on you no more than four *leguas* from Son-oyta?"

Longarm didn't point out just how much the older man had given away about his authority over the remote station. It was his own fault for not fibbing more carefully earlier.

The gal brought Longarm more *pulque,* and sat across from him with a mug of her own as he polished off the ham and eggs surprised at how hungry he seemed to be after all.

He didn't have to pay all that much attention to the plump and lonesome *mestiza* to sense she was what her own kind defined as *nada más sube el culo.* But he wasn't in the market for an easy lay. He had to get to Puerto Peñasco, better than fifty miles away, before those crooks he couldn't identify on sight put Harmony Drake and that bitch Goldmine Gloria aboard that coastal steamer bound for Yuma.

He knew they were backtracking to Yuma now. Aside from the steamboat connection they seemed to be aiming for, the whole bunch would be able to fade into the wood-work faster north of the border. That was doubtless why they'd gone to so much trouble to convince everyone they were bound for the paradise of El Presidénte Diaz, with its gringo-baiting, brutal, itchy-trigger-fingered lawmen.

The plump and discontented gal drinking *pulque* with

him broke into his thoughts by asking if he meant to hire a room out back for the night, or whether he might be interested in an arrangement that would cost him no more than a few gestures of kindness to a poor *mujer* who'd been driven almost to *manájarad*.

Longarm had to laugh as he considered the time he'd gotten himself into an even sillier conversation in Laredo by confusing the verb *manejar,* meaning to manage or drive, with *manájar*, meaning to jack off.

The gal took his lighthearted expression more romantically than intended. But it would have been needlessly cruel to a gal who seemed to mean well had he flatly refused when she suggested he finish his snack and let her show him around out back.

Longarm knew Marshal Billy Vail had never sent him all this way to fool around with Mexican gals, or even Mexico, so he explained he had to get on down the road because moonlight made for cooler riding than sunlight in a Sonora August.

She favored him with a Mona Lisa smile and demurely asked if he really thought he could last the night with a woman of passion who'd been feeling neglected since she'd broken up with a certain blacksmith. Longarm laughed again despite himself, and she quickly added that they had to wait for Tio Hector, her boss, to settle down for the night in any case.

She said, "Is still early. If you wait until after ten you can go with God, my eternal gratitude, and those fresh mounts you asked him for in vain, eh?"

Longarm raised an eyebrow and quietly asked, "You could get away with that . . . ah . . . ?"

"My friends call me Ampollita," she confided, rising from their table to reach for his hand as she added, "We shall have to, how you say, take care of the *establero* in charge of the remuda, since he and he alone keeps exact figures on the mules that come and go. You see, we exchange one team of six spent mules for a team of fresh ones every time a coach arrives from either direction. Then there are the extra ones we must keep on hand for to be sure, in case we get a lamed one for to water, feed, and rest. So . . .''

"I know how you run a stage line," Longarm told her. "How much will I have to slip your head wrangler for those fresh mules?"

She shrugged her bare shoulders and demurely replied, "*Quien sabe*? He may feel that sorrel can be disposed of in town for enough to repay the favor. Let me argue the point with him later. He speaks no English."

Longarm allowed he could manage enough Spanish for some horse trading. But Ampollita pulled him to his feet, with a surprising strength, and told him, "A third party can always strike the better bargain for you. Is easier for to lie when nobody can ask trick questions, such as where did one buy such a mount in the first place."

That cinched it. The jolly little thing seemed to know more than she was letting on, and Billy Vail would want him to question her in more depth, as long as he wasn't exactly torturing her.

He repeated what he'd said about not having all night, and she again assured him nobody was expecting that much out of him. Then she asked him to shut up as she led him out an archway and along a dark corridor lined with mysterious doorways.

She allowed it was safe to talk again once they'd entered a 'dobe cell at the far end and she'd bolted the heavy oaken door behind them.

He said, "Nice place you got here," as he stared around at the four walls crowding the only furnishings, a pine washstand and a fair-sized bedstead for these parts. A row of carved wooden *santos* stared severely down at them from plank shelf facing the foot of the bed.

She saw what he was staring at and giggled, saying, "It

is about *time* they answered my prayers, no?''

Then she hauled the blouse off over her black curls, and dropped her ample skirts around her ankles to simply step out of them, as well as her braided leather *sandalias*, and stand there, hands on hips in the candlelight, asking how he liked it so far.

He gulped and allowed she'd make a fortune posing for an art class in Paris, France, provided she'd learn to hold still a bit. But she was bumping and grinding with a wicked smile on her pretty but sort of coarse face by the time Longarm had propped the Big Fifty in one corner and gotten himself undressed.

So he was showing it hard as he stepped out of his pants and moved to join her. He'd figured on lowering her to the bedding, but she said she liked it better standing up, and swung her bare back and ample behind to face the smooth oaken door as Longarm just followed the head of his turgid organ-grinder where they both wanted it to go.

He had to spread his own legs wider to lower his center of gravity as Ampollita gasped, *"Ay, Dios mio, que grande! Chinge me! Chinge me mucho, El Brazo Largo!"*

He did. Most men would have. But it almost went soft on him when that shit about him being El Brazo Largo sank in. He reached down to hook an elbow under either of her plump bare knees and slide her up the oak paneling to pound her big soft rump against the door with his own legs straight. She found it more comfortable too, judging by the feline sounds coming out of her as she clung tightly to him inside and out, while he shot his wad inside her.

She sighed, ''I felt that and I am so happy, El Brazo Largo!''

He left it in her, but stopped moving as he quietly replied, ''So am I. But could we keep it down to a roar, and how did you ever get the notion I was this Largo gent, *mi corazón*?''

She said she was still too excited for talk, and suggested

they do something less tiring aboard her bedstead. He figured that would be a better place to talk. So a good time was had by all as he enjoyed her again with one of the pillows under her gyrating hips while she boxed his ears with her bare feet every time he slowed down. It was easier to see, in this position, how she had been getting more satisfaction in the kitchen than in bed. From the way she was sweating and gasping as she did at least two thirds of the work, he felt certain he'd just helped her shed a few pounds. He knew *he* was getting hungry again. It seemed a swell way to stay in shape, if only it didn't make you come so soon whenever it got this good!

He finally had her calmed down enough to answer questions as he lit a cheroot to share with her on top of the rumpled sheets. She said it was well known that El Brazo Largo rode with the rebel leader, El Gato, and that everyone knew El Gato's band was somewhere in Sonora at the moment because so many *rurales* and *federales* were concentrated over to the east right now.

He let her have a drag on their cheroot as he soberly observed she sure seemed to make up her pretty head at short notice. He said, "I've heard a tall gringo with a mustache has been seen in the company of El Gato on occasion. Since you called El Gato a rebel instead of a bandit, I'd hazard a guess you don't share your Tio Hector's political opinions. But a heap of us old West-by-God-Virginia boys grew up long and lean to grow some hair on our fool faces."

Ampollita snuggled closer and put the cheroot to Longarm's lips as she confided, "Everyone here, save for the old fool in charge, prays for the fall of Diaz and La Causa de Libertad. I guessed at who you had to be because you rode in on that sorrel, with those four notches carved on the handle of that six-shooter, eh?"

Longarm snorted, "*Mierda*, I never cut those fool

notches on that old army thumb-buster. It came my way like so."

She said, "I know. The two riders you must have met before you got here stopped by a day or so ago. The one who was carrying the same six-shooter was riding a palomino. After they had eaten, and left us unharmed, Tio Hector sent a rider for to tell *los rurales* anyway. He said they were *banditos* he had read about in the newspapers. Later on, *los rurales* told us not to worry, because they knew the two of them were headed for El Norte for to rob a gringo trading post and blame it on Los Indios."

"Great minds run in the same channels," Longarm sighed as the coy cantina gal toyed with his damp pubic hairs. He chanced saying, "*Esta bien*, I did meet up with those two ambitious *banditos*, and it would be false modesty to say they won. But why does that have to make me this wild and woolly gringo who rides with Mexican rebels?"

She answered simply, "Because you won. They were not a pair of schoolchildren out for to have some fun. They were well-known killers. Both of them. When we saw one man alone had helped himself to one of their mounts and pistols, we knew he had to be *better*. So what do you get when you add up a deadly tall Anglo with a mustache and admiration for El Gato, when you know El Gato is riding nearby, and—"

"You said *we*," Longarm cut in, demanding, "Who's we, Ampollita?"

She shrugged and said, "*La raza*, here at this *fonda*. Tio Hector told one of the *muchachos* for to ride into Sonoyta and tell *los rurales* you were stranded here with jaded mounts."

Longarm gasped, "Kee-rist, it's about *time* you told me! Were you telling the truth about being able to fix me up with fresh mounts?"

She sighed and said, "*No se preocupe, querido*. I told

the *muchacho* for to ride slow. Nobody but Tio Hector would wish for to make El Gato cross with them. I shall have you on your way in no time. But first do it to me one more time for to steady my nerves when *los rurales* arrive."

Chapter 8

So Ampollita's nerves were likely steadier than Longarm's as he rode by moonlight with fresh mules carrying the same loads at a brisker pace.

He was tempted to push them faster to make up the time he'd lost—it had hardly been wasted—at the roadside *fonda*. He forced himself to take it slow but steady, knowing there was just no way he was going to make it in to Puerto Peñasco before daybreak or, hell, in one jump. The fugitives would have to hole up in such shade as they could manage for most of the coming day and push on to the Sea of Cortez the following night. If Ampollita had been right about that Yuma-bound coastal steamer, things might work out even better if he got in just before the fugitives boarded it.

He thought he'd heard something in the distance, and reined in for a tighter listen. The night sky wasn't as easy to keep time by as his missing pocket watch, but he figured they were better than two hours south of that *fonda* now. So what sure sounded like hoofbeats, a lot of hoofbeats, was coming from somewhere closer.

"Those *rurales* made good time from Sonoyta, didn't they?" he asked his mules in a disgusted tone as he dismounted to lead the two of them off the road towards the moon so everything would be outlined in the same shade of blackness. He led on foot to choose his path with care. A furlong out, he tethered both mules behind the same clump of organpipe and told them he'd be right back.

As he and the Big Fifty moved toward the road again, he looked back the way he'd just come, and saw nothing much but organpipes, separated just enough to peer between, rising higher than either mule.

On the way back to the moonlit road Longarm got out that knife from the trading post and cut a willowy branch of paloverde. When he met up with the sign he and the mules had left in the pale crust as they'd left the trail, he cradled the Big Fifty in one arm and got busy with his improvised broom. He swept sign to where hardly anyone but a desert Indian, scouting hard in the moonlight on foot, was likely to notice a slightly darker and rougher patch of caliche. He kept at it as he crawfished back between some cardon and prickle-pear. He'd chosen that gap through the cactus with exactly this move in mind.

Once he'd crawfished that far, he figured they'd either spot sign and rein in or they wouldn't. So he moved on back to the mules and stood between them with the rifle braced in the organpipe clump that made a better screen than a fort. As those other critters got nearer, at a brisk trot, Longarm put a palm over either mule's velvety muzzle, but didn't pinch any nostrils just yet. Mounts could be divided into those who nickered at strangers and those who didn't. A nose bag or gentle palm seemed to have a calming effect. If gentle methods failed, neither a horse nor mule could breathe through its mouth, and like anyone else, they had to take a deep breath before they let out a serious yell.

A low, calm voice had a quieting effect as well. So Longarm softly told them, "Sounds like six or eight riders, stirrup to stirrup and serious as hell about getting there. The next stage stop to the south figures to offer them remounts, whether they want to or not, if those are *rurales* out for blood!''

But it wasn't. Longarm had to laugh at his own sense of drama as he saw the bulky dark mass of a stagecoach swaying southward, with no running lights lit, behind its six-mule team.

He watched with a wistful smile as it rattled and rumbled past at a pace he could only envy. He told his own mules, ''They'll have made it to the next *fonda* and a change of teams before midnight, with time out for everyone to coffee and shit whilst the three of us plod on at a trail pace. They'll likely make it all the way in to Puerto Peñasco by the time we're scouting for some shade a night's ride short!''

He began to swap loads as he heard the coach rattle and rumble out of earshot. He muttered, ''Just as well I never waited for that late-running coach. Lord knows why it's running so late, and I'd already been spotted as a wanted man by others working for the same outfit.''

He untethered, mounted up, and led off at an angle through the moonlight, drifting back towards the road, as he assured himself he knew what he was doing.

He lit a smoke, cupping the match flame in his palm. Then he held the lit cheroot in a cupped hand, army style, instead of between his teeth. Smoking at times and in places you weren't supposed to didn't really make your forbidden treat taste better. But it gave you something to do and kept you wide awake.

Back on the road again, where he'd be harder to trail, Longarm mentally paced off the ride ahead, and saw that while there was no hope of making it in what was left of this night, he'd be riding in before midnight tomorrow night. That would still be early for a Mexican seaport.

He told his mule, ''I'll find a good home for you kids. Then I'll use the ill-gotten gains of those bandits to buy me most everything I lost, save for my badge.''

He snorted angry smoke out both nostrils and grumbled,

"I'll get my badge and the bunch of them! They won't want to board that boat to Yuma until it's fixing to shove off. So if I get aboard it earlier I can . . . Great day in the morning, I don't have to do *shit*! Not if all of us are aboard, but they don't know it, before we steam through the delta and U.S. Customs comes aboard at Yuma!"

He laughed mockingly and nodded in passing to a solemn old saguaro. "Howdy, U.S. Customs. I'd be U.S. Deputy Marshal Custis Long of the Denver District Court, and I'd surely be obliged if you all would help me make some federal arrests aboard this vessel!"

The saguaro didn't laugh. Longarm warned himself to stop jawing out loud like a prisoner jerking off in a solitary cell. The night noises all about sounded louder, and spookier, once he had.

He'd read somewhere that mankind, having eyes that worked better by daylight, had invented bad dreams and ghost stories to keep everyone huddled safer after dark instead of wandering about, half blind, to step off a cliff or into something bigger, hungrier, and with better night vision. It still beat all how uneasy an elf owl could make one feel, even when one knew that was only a bitty owl-bird calling from a woodpecker's hollow in a saguaro.

The crickets chirping all about could spook a night rider worse. Desert crickets didn't chirp any spookier than the ones you might hear by the hearth of some old run-down house. They spooked you by suddenly stopping for long pregnant pauses, every time someone or something else as big as a fool kit fox, or something meaner, passed within yards of the bugs. You seldom heard real rattlesnakes late at night in the desert. But there were all sorts of other critters who seemed to delight in buzzing like an eight-foot diamondback to scare you shitless and spook your mount. One breed of grasshopper had that sudden sinister buzz down pat. It could spook your mount just as much.

But the mules Ampollita had sent him on his way aboard

91

were used to this very road at night, and happy to be driven down it at a far more gentle pace than they were used to. He'd find out how they felt about taking him more than ten or twelve miles without getting the rest of the night off when they got to the next *fonda* down the road. He didn't aim to stop there, or even let the folks inside get a good look at him. For sooner or later that message from the first *fonda*'s boss had to reach *los rurales*, and it was always best to let such a swell bunch just *guess* which way you'd gone for certain.

He'd trot them a furlong, walk them two, and rein in for a breather now and again, changing mounts when he stopped for a real trail break every ninety minutes or so. Hence he figured he was setting a pace of at least a third of the cross-country speed of that night coach, and so it didn't seem astounding when he suddenly realized the next stage stop was just down the road a piece, 'dobe walls and high *mirador* or lookout tower barely visible in the moonlight, and nary a speck of candle glow to greet them.

"Must be after four in the morning, so they're all asleep," he told his mules as he reined to a walk, considering the sounds of all eight hooves in the moonlit dust.

No dogs were barking. No window shutters were being thrown open, and sneaking through cactus and stickerbrush far enough out to matter, seemed the slower way to Puerto Peñasco. So he decided to just ease on by.

He almost managed. Then, just as he drew abreast of a roadside window, a female voice on the edge of total hysteria called out in high-toned Spanish, "*Quien es? Que desea? No tengo dinero, pero tengo fusiles.*"

Longarm reined in again to calmly assure the frightened lady he was only a poor wayfaring stranger, he didn't want anything, and he had his own money and guns if it was all the same with her.

She must have noticed his accent. She called out, "*E usted Americano?* Oh, that is true. They told me one of E

Gato's followers is a gringo! There is nothing left here for to steal, and I warn you I will shoot if you come any closer!''

Longarm calmly replied, "In that case I'd best be on my way then, seeing I make you feel so tense. But just to satisfy my own curious nature, Señorita, are you saying you all have been pestered by El Gato and some other gringo? I'm missing something here. I thought El Gato led a rebel band, and hadn't heard he'd been recruiting all that many of *my* kind. I hate to have to admit it, but not many gringo riders of the Owlhoot Trail share El Gato's idealistic notions. Neither Frank nor Jesse act as much like old Robin Hood as they would have us all believe.''

The unseen woman, who might or might not have had a gun trained on Longarm, said uncertainly, "I do not understand the point you seem to make. I do not know much more about what has been going on at this *fonda*. I came in aboard the mail coach to Puerto Peñasco a few hours ago. We were running late because there was talk of El Gato's band out our way and everybody knows he likes to strike in the dark, like the mouser he is named for.''

Longarm quietly replied, "Hardly seems fair to say your stage was stopped by El Gato unless you saw him *do* it, Señorita.''

She said, "I just told you I was confused. The coach crew cursed when they drove in to find nobody here for to change their team for them. While they were arguing about what to do about that, I excused myself for to use the . . . *letrina*. When I returned, they had driven on without waiting for me. I think they must have been very frightened of something. From the way this place was deserted, with coals in the kitchen stove still glowing, something must have frightened everyone. I know that *I* am most frightened. I am called Consuela O'Hara y Mendez, and you are called . . . ?''

"My friends call me Custis, Custis Crawford,'' Longarm

93

lied, since most of the high-toned families down this way sided with Diaz to begin with, and since it was easy to recall how kissing-cousin Crawford Long had come up with ether anesthesia in time to save a heap of old boys a heap of pain at places such as Shiloh and Cold Harbor. Then Longarm told the lady peering out the window at him that he had to get on down the road.

She sobbed, "*Espere!* Do not leave me here alone in the desert!"

Longarm looked eastward at the first faint hint of dawn as he told her, "I wish you'd make up your mind, Miss Consuela. I have to find some safe shade for these mules and me before the sun comes up. For those unwinking stars up yonder ain't forecasting a cold spell. I got a spare mule if you ain't too fat, and while we're at it, is there any spare water to be had in yonder?"

She eagerly told him about the well pumps behind the kitchen and empty stable out back. So he dismounted and led both mules in through the overhang of the fortress-like walls of the quarters and stable, to find the stranded *señorita* waiting for him in the courtyard.

He couldn't say how pretty she might be in such faint moonlight, but he could see she was young and filled her cotton summer dress in a refined willowy way. He wasn't surprised to see she didn't really have a gun.

He ticked his hat brim to her. Then he led the mules to the watering trough by the stable entrance, pumped it half full, and let them both go at it.

He explained he'd been husbanding his trail water, and explained how she'd have to share one mule with topped off water bags and ride bareback. She said she knew how to ride, but asked, "For why do you wish for to push on with sunrise almost upon us? Do you know of a safer place, with more shade, than this *fonda*?"

To which he could only reply, "I sure do. There's thirty or forty miles of open desert betwixt here and Puerto Peñ asco, with all sorts of shady stuff to be found along the way if you really look hard for it. I know this deserted *fonda* has shade, water, and walls as thick as the ones at the Alamo. I've heard it said that Travis and Bowie were still dumb to wait, since Santa Anna was sure to come looking for 'em.''

The marooned Mexican gal said, "*Los rurales* are as likely to come along as those bandits, no?''

Longarm didn't want to argue politics with a lady who seemed that enthusiastic about *rurales*. So he just shrugged and replied, ''It'll be way safer if it's left for us to decide who we want to wave to along this mighty lonesome road, Miss Consuela. You can stay here if you'd rather. I can't say for certain whether you'd be safer either way. I don't know what scared a whole bunch of grown men to flee these thick walls, all this water, and like you said, a road out front patrolled now and again by *rurales*. I figure it must have been something sort of scary. I'd rather not wait here and see if it comes back.''

She allowed how, in that case, she'd just as soon tag along. -

Leaving the mules to laze in the moonlit courtyard, Longarm and his newfound traveling companion went into the *fonda* to fetch her one carpetbag and see if the others had left anything useful behind in their sudden stampede for safer ground.

Longarm lit a wall sconce inside to shed some light on the subject. He was glad he had as soon as he saw what Consuela O'Hara y Mendez really looked like.

Aside from looking worried, the obviously Irish and Spanish gal of perhaps twenty-five had wavy auburn hair to go with her big blue eyes. But her skin, exposed from the breastbone up, was that odd soft shade of peach you almost never saw on anyone but certain gals from the olive-growing parts of Spain.

She'd left her baggage out front in the taproom. Longarm

moved back to the kitchen with a view to grabbing at least a sack of cracked corn or frijoles for the mules. He lit a waterproof Mexican match made more like a small candle than a wooden stick, and found an oil lamp near the kitchen sink. He lit that too. Then he stared harder at the plastered 'dobe above the sink and muttered, "Aw, shit."

Someone had written *"Yaqui!"* with a finger dipped in chili sauce, or blood. That was all Longarm needed as he blew out the lamp and stode out to rejoin Consuela, saying, *"Vamos. En seguida.* I'll explain along the way."

He did. It was easy, as he got Consuela and their combined baggage, including eighty pounds of fresh water, loaded up. You didn't have to explain as much about Yaqui to a gal who'd been raised on a ranch in these parts.

The Yaqui Indians of Northwest Mexico claimed to be left-over Aztecs who'd never surrendered to the Spanish, and acted as if they were out to take Mexico back in the name of Montezuma.

As advanced as Pueblo when it came to raising corn, beans, and kids in their canyon strongholds, the Yaqui were better than Apache when it came to raising hell. They'd have been as famous as Apache, Sioux, and such had they raised hell north of the border. But fortunately for most Anglo soldiers and settlers, the Yaqui raided close to home and the Mexican newspapers tended to play down all the embarrassment they caused Mexico's official Indian policy.

Mexican governments, all the way back to those of Old Spain, held that the best way to get along with Indians was by fair but firm, if not exactly gentle, persuasion.

Instead of setting up a Bureau of Indian Affairs, old Cortez and the governors who'd come after him had simply ordered any Indians he hadn't already killed to wipe off that fool paint, put on Christian pants, and show up for the early Mass at the nearest mission church.

The policy had worked as well as Uncle Sam's, at less cost to both sides in the end, with *most* of Mexico's native population. It was tougher to hold an Indian uprising when so many Indians had Spanish kith or kin, and vice versa. But not unlike some snooty white folks to the north, the Yaqui didn't hold with marrying up or even shaking hands with anyone who didn't speak their Nahuatlan version of Uto-Aztec and pray to the same bloody-minded elder gods of Old Mexico.

Having agreed they wanted nothing to do with any Yaqui, Longarm and the stranded Mexican gal lit out down the road until it was getting light enough to see colors.

Then Longarm led them off along a gentle ridge, pointing to a distant clump of mesquite as he called back, "Those mesquite seem to be sprouting from black basalt rock. Might be an old volcanic plug. Even if it ain't, mesquite offers more shade than anything else out this way and the mules can browse it, if they're careful about the thorns."

She allowed there was plenty of mesquite on her husband's ranch. That was the first Longarm had heard of any damned old husband. He hadn't noticed her wearing any damned old ring, and that was the second thing a man looked for, once he'd admired a gal's form and face.

It was hardly the time to ask where her mysterious husband might be. So he just led on to get them all under the low canopy of feathery mesquite leaves, greened up by that recent rain, and discover that, as he'd hoped, the center of the grove was a dirt-filled hollow surrounded by a two-or three-foot natural fortress of rounded basalt boulders.

He helped her down and began to unload the mules he'd tethered on long leads to separate mesquite trunks, explaining as he did so, "I read how they get formations like this in the dry country of South Africa too. Only you don't find *diamonds* out our way. Columns of lava cool, shrink, and crack underground. Ground water rots out the centers a tad faster, the way a big old tree stump might rot, as the winds and rains peel away the original grade to . . . Well, you were looking for a safer place to spend the day, not a geology lecture. So suffice it to say we've found shade, a wide-open field of fire all around, and a swell place to fire from.''

She stared about nervously in the tricky light of a harsh desert sunrise as she asked who might be creeping up on them out there in the middle of nowhere.

He answered, ''Likely nobody, Miss Consuela. I left that coach road on what was almost a sudden impulse when I noticed it was passing through a ridge with lots of slickrock and little deep caliche. We had to leave sign hither and yon along those three furlongs of ridge we just now negotiated. But like you say, it looks like the middle of nowhere and nobody has any call to expect us over here in this common-looking clump of mesquite. So what say I unroll some bedding and let you recline with some tomato preserves for a lie-down breakfast?''

She looked sort of shocked, but managed a polite smile as she told him it was not that she didn't feel grateful to him for having rescued her from that frightening situation, but that he had to give her time to think.

She said, ''Is true I have left Carlos forever, having caught him doing vile things with a mere servant. Maybe I *did* say I would do the same vile things with the first handsome man I met back in Ciudad Mejico, for I was most hurt as well as angry. But I was not expecting a handsome *gringo*, and I feel suddenly awkward about going to bed with you.''

Longarm smiled thinly and demanded, ''Who said anything about me going to bed with anybody? Don't *I* have anything to say about it? Is that all you women ever think about?''

She blinked owlishly up and him, suddenly laughed like hell, and said she'd always heard that worked the other way around.

To which Longarm could only reply, ''Maybe it does,

other times and places. Right now I figure we're a day's ride from help in any direction, with the Yaqui on the rise a heap closer. So if it's all the same with you, Miss Consuela, I mean to keep this Big Fifty in my arms instead of you or even Miss Ellen Terry. For, no offense, neither of you gals, pretty as I find you both, can spit six hundred grains of lead half as far!''

Chapter 9

Longarm had read those unwinking desert stars all too right. It was pushing a hundred in the shade before noon, and the sun-lashed desert all around was shimmering as if behind a rain-washed window pane, while a shimmering silvery sea, or a mighty realistic mirage, now covered the coach road and the dry land beyond as far as some nameless ridge of shattered bedrock.

He'd gotten Consuela to stretch out atop a flannel blanket in her thin silk dress. She'd even dozed off more than once for a hot and sweaty catnap. But then she'd wake up to drone some more about her awful love life.

Longarm had long since noticed that when it came to screwing, men couldn't think of much else they'd rather do, and women couldn't think of much else thing they'd rather talk about—especially when it just wasn't practical to really *do* it. So Longarm was commencing to feel left out as she went on and on about all those other men who'd used and abused her during an adult life that hardly seemed long enough.

To hear Consuela tell it, she'd been sent off to a convent school after her momma caught a wicked but hardly cruel

100

stepfather feeling for pubic hair where none had sprouted as yet.

She'd felt for it herself a lot, and run off with a handsome groundskeeper at the precocious age of thirteen. So the same stepdad who'd fooled with her earlier had had the peon love of her life shot for trespassing. Then, since her momma found her awkward to have around the house, they'd married her off young to a rich as well as dirty old man. She'd found some of his advanced notions about the ways of a man with a maid delightfully exciting. He'd found her such a delight in bed that he'd died there, leaving her a rich young widow.

She said, "I never should have married Carlos a year later. He was only after my money and not, alas, my body. He said La Santa Fe forbade all but one position, and so I steeled myself to accept my lackluster lot. But then I caught him in the position of sixty-nine on the floor tiles, with a cleaning woman of mixed blood!"

Longarm suppressed a yawn and said, "Some men seem to like a bowl of chili after they've been dining on steak for a spell. I hope you had the sense to get your money out of there before you lit out in person aboard that night coach."

She sighed and replied, "I wired my bank for to transfer my account to Puerto Peñasco two days before I left, while Carlos was away on business, or with some *puta*, the beast."

Longarm stared thoughtfully at some seagulls floating on the sea over yonder as he cocked a brow and asked, "You can *wire* south to the capital and across to the Sea of Cortez from that dinky border town? No offense, but I ain't seen many telegraph poles along that coach road to the east. None sticking out of all that mirage either."

She explained how the telegraph line ran a more direct course to Mexico City and from there to the west coast. She didn't have to tell him why the nationalized telegraph network had to avoid some parts of a north infested with unreconstructed Indians and bitterly poor mixed bloods. But she told him anyway.

He found it felt better to chew on a mesquite stem than a smoke when it got this hot and dry. So he was doing so as he sighed and observed, half to himself, "*Los rurales* in Sonoyta will have wired ahead to Puerto Peñasco by now. then. They wear those big gray felt sombreros as a rule, right?"

She nodded. "*Es verdad*, but for why would *los rurales* take any interest in my leaving Carlos?"

Longarm smiled thinly and replied, "You're right. I'm likely just worrying over nothing. Them four *white* sombreros out yonder wouldn't be *los rurales* or even honest *vaqueros* at this hour of the morning on such a dazzling day."

Consuela sat up to peer off to the east the same way, sounding a bit like a little kid as she marveled, "Ooh, *el miraje!* But I see no sombreros of any color out there. Do we seem to be underwater to them as well?"

Longarm morosely replied, "They must see *something* over this way. That's likely why they're heading so directly at us. Watch what seems to be bitty white dots near that three-branched saguaro. All those bitty dots are shimmering in the rising heat waves, but only the four white ones are moving closer."

She gasped, "*Ay, Dios mio!* I see what you mean! I hope they are not those savage Yaqui!"

Longarm sighed and said, "So do I. It ain't my fight, and some of the Yaqui I've convinced of that treated me tolerable enough. It's the ones I can't seem to convince that I try to avoid. As friend or foe, your average Yaqui seems more emotional than your average gent of any other breed."

He smiled wistfully at the memory of a lean brown Yaqui gal it wouldn't have been decent to brag about, and continued. "I savvy just a few words of the more northern dialects of their overall lingo. A Papago can understand a Hopi or Shoshoni about as well as a Spaniard could follow the drift of a Portuguese or Italian. But every time I've tried that on Yaqui, they answer in Spanish and tell me not to mock 'em. I reckon it's something like the way you folks feel about high-toned Castilian and Border Mex."

She told him in a worried tone not to worry about that, and asked if he knew how to tell Yaqui in Spanish that some of her best friends were Indians.

He chuckled dryly and replied, "If they're willing to talk first. I've found it best to just dodge 'em when they're on the war path. We ain't close enough to their home range in the Sierra Madre for them to be picking flowers."

She looked wildly about, her unbound hair whipping like burnished telegraph wire, as she asked which way they could ride to dodge those ominous white dots.

He wearily replied, "I just said that." Then he rose to his feet to take up a new position a few feet closer to the line of the higher ground they'd followed to this rare patch of shade.

Consuela moved to join him as he calmly took a half-dozen long .50-120-600 rounds from their belt loops and lined them neatly in front of him on the black rock of the low natural barricade. He braced the Big Fifty to one side and laid the Schofield .45 Short by the cartridges on the rock as he said, "Maybe they're only bandits, or even better, just making for that coach road betwixt us and them. They won't spot any sign we left as long as they don't cross the road to make for this shade."

She asked what the odds of them doing that might be.

He sighed and said, "It's pushing noon and they'd be fixing to hole up for *la siesta* if they were back wherever they've come from. I'm fixing to fire my first round wide, as a warning. Anyone at all familiar with the rules of the Owlhoot Trail ought to follow my drift. If they're innocent travelers, they'll ride on and look for their own damned shade. If they don't, we'll know it's open season on such rude gents.''

She said she knew how to handle a pistol. To which he could only reply, ''That would be swell if you had one. We're going to have to cover both sides of this teeny mesquite grove if my first ruse don't work. But right now I need both these guns, great and small.''

Before he had to explain further, the sun had risen another notch in the cloudless cobalt sky and what had seemed a vast shimmering sea just wasn't there anymore.

The four widely spaced riders hadn't vanished, though. At this still-wavering distance it was impossible to say whether they were Mexicans of the ruder sort or Indians who'd taken those advances they'd found useful while rejecting sissy notions such as property rights or the right of any stranger to go on breathing.

Longarm waited until the four of them got to the road and bunched closer around the one pointing directly at him and Consuela—or at least at the shade they were sweating in. Then Longarm sighed and picked up the pistol, saying, ''I fear we're about to have company. If they're Indians they'll read two mules heading out this way. Let 'em get halfway along the ridge and then call out to them to ask 'em nicely to go away.''

She asked, ''Will that not alert them to the fact that one of us is a woman?''

He nodded grimly and explained. ''When you're down to your last chips you play the cards you hold. Tempting as the thought of your used and abused body might be to anyone who's yet to lay eyes on the same, I don't want 'em thinking one gun is *alone* out here with a pack mule. You yell. Then I'll yell at you to shut up. That ought to make them study on bothering to circle us in this heat, seeing two or more of us could be watching both ways with any number of guns, see?''

She didn't seem to. He didn't have time to elaborate. The four mystery riders had tethered a roan, a buckskin, and two paints near the road to ease along the low ridge afoot through the knee-high brittlebush. There was a clump of taller organpipe a furlong or a little over two town blocks off. Longarm told Consuela to challenge them just as they drew abreast of the cactus screen.

She did, calling out, *"Váyesen! No me jodas, cabrones!"*

Longarm had to laugh as the four of them took cover. For such a high-toned little gal, Consuela had quite a mouth on her. Having no improvements to add, he called out in English, "Don't fuck with *me* either, you dumb jerk-offs!"

He was answered only by dead silence. He picked up the Schofield and pegged a shot low toward that clump of organpipe.

Consuela saw the puff of dust, and sadly observed the underpowered pistol didn't have that much range.

He grinned wolfishly and replied, "As a matter of fact, I *could* lob some slow-moving .45 Short slugs that far, if distance was all I was aiming for. I ain't out to *hit* anybody with this six-gun. I only want them to know we have it, and that we were serious about wanting them to ride on and leave us alone."

A blur of dusty white showed itself for an instant between some low stickerbush closer than those organpipes. She gasped, and Longarm said, "I see him. Two are hunkered behind that screen of cactus. The other two are trying to sidewind closer. They figure they're still well out of range."

Then he emptied the wheel of the Schofield their way to give them pause, and reloaded it as he soberly explained, "They are, if this was all we had at our disposal. I want you to move over to the far side of the mules with this and cover our rear. I don't think they're out to circle us just yet. I think they're planning on waiting, just outside of range, until dark. But you never know what Yaqui might be up to. They like to surprise you."

She took the Schofield gingerly, but asked if the Indians weren't likely to fry their brains out under the hot son of an entire afternoon in August.

He said, "Their brains don't work like yours or mine. Get cracking with that gun, and don't fire it unless your target is closer than you'd ever want a Yaqui to get!"

She sounded as if she might be crying as she moved off through the dappled shade. Longarm didn't feel like crying, but he sure felt alone.

Then he sighed and said, "Well, you were warned polite that you weren't welcome here."

Knowing at least one was nearer, with farther to run, Longarm drew a bead on that cactus clump halfway to the road and fired.

He was reloading without looking out for results as the echoes of his first Big Fifty shot were still fading. He'd reloaded as that one who'd been creeping closer jumped to his feet, yelling like a she-wolf giving birth to busted glass, and ran towards the smoking buffalo gun instead of away.

Yaqui were like that.

"You poor brave kid!" Longarm sighed, just before he pulled the trigger to blow the charging Indian's left lung and shoulder blade out his back with a bucket of blood. Then he was reloading, as fast as he was able, and he still barely made it as another, wearing only white pants and sombrero, rose from behind some brittlebush to take careful aim Longarm's way with a muzzle-loader left over from the Mexican War.

Longarm fired first. So it was never established whether the Yaqui had known what he was up to or not. It was said a Yaqui was harder to stop with a bullet than most. But a slug meant to knock a bull buffalo down seemed to do the trick.

Then Consuela was screaming and blazing away with that Schofield. So Longarm was up and reloading on the run. He joined her on the far side of the grove as the mules brayed and shook the mesquite branches above them. The Yaqui tearing up the open slope with a wild grin and a waving machete, despite the blood running down his side, seemed even wilder until Longarm dropped him with a second, much bigger hunk of hot lead.

He reloaded and put a second round into the limp form to make sure. Then he handed Consuela some spare .45 Shorts and said, "Nice going. Reload and keep up the good work whilst I tidy up out front."

He got back to the buffalo rounds still spread on the rocks just in time to see the fourth surviving Yaqui trotting reluctantly toward those distant ponies three furlongs or better than six hundred yards away. Hence out of rifle range, or so he must have thought.

So the Indian was turning his head to grin back as hot metal slammed into his ear to tear his face off and skim his straw sombrero off like a pie plate.

Longarm reloaded and got up to call Consuela in, saying, "I counted four coming in and we seem to have put four on the ground. Wait here and I'll fetch those sunbaked ponies."

He did. But it wasn't that easy. For as he broke cover, the fatally shot first one rose to his knees in the blood-spattered cotton to draw a wavering bead on Longarm and take another buffalo round where it seemed best to shoot a Yaqui, smack between the eyes.

Over by the organpipe clump, Longarm found that one staring up at the cloudless sky with a sleepy smile, his white shirt spattered with red blood and green cactus pulp. There was nothing worth taking from the faceless horror closer to the road either.

The four ponies, brands and saddles indicating they'd been taken from some unfortunate Mexicans, had to be led wide of all the fresh-spilled blood. But they greeted Consuela and the two mules as if they'd known them for many a year.

As Longarm watered the overheated ponies, he told Consuela there wasn't enough for all of them in those five-gallon bags.

He said, "I can cut and pulp some cactus. Pear is all right and barrel is better, for the stock. We'll save the well water for the two of *us*. Come sundown, we'd better turn the mules loose on yonder road. They're coach mules who know it well. They'll make it to the nearest *fonda* that's still pumping water. You and me ought to make it on out of this desert in one hard night's ride, changing back and fourth with four mighty tough ponies."

She asked how he could tell how tough their brand-new mounts were.

He answered simply, "Yaqui were riding 'em. Horse Indians sort of go along with Professor Darwin when it comes to choosing horseflesh. If a pony can take 'em where they want to go, when they want to get there, they keep it as a mount. When it can't, they eat it. We ain't got time to talk about it. We have to get far from here fast. I'd best see now about that cactus water. I vote we leave here just after sundown, and this ain't no parliamentary democracy. We'd best shun that road everyone knows about and beeline by moonlight across the caliche. We'll be leaving a mighty easy trail to follow as we do so. But that won't matter if we've made it out of this fool desert before it's light enough for any other Yaqui or . . . bandits to follow."

She didn't argue. He broke out some more canned grub and opened it for her before he stepped back out in the blast-furnace glare with a gunnysack to gather some cactus pads.

They were in luck. He found more than one watermelon-sized barrel cactus along with some soapier-tasting pear.

He toted them all back to the shade, where Consuela watched with interest as he got all the well water into one rubberized bag before he began to refill the empty one with cactus juice.

As he did so, he explained. "Found what was left of a wagon party surrounded by this barrel cactus one time. It appeared they'd died of thirst, the poor greenhorns. None of 'em could have known there was a few quarts of tolerable water in each and every one of these thorny things. Thanks to that recent rain, these are juicier than usual. So their pulp water's almost pure."

She asked for a pear pad to cut up as salad greens for their pork and beans. He didn't care. It was sort of a cross between lettuce and soap suds when you weren't used to it. But being a Mexican, she was used to it. He allowed he'd have some too. For the more moisture you got in you the better, especially when you couldn't tell how much you'd really sweated since your last good whistle-wetting.

It got hotter. Consuela said she couldn't believe that was possible either, and she'd been living in Sonora a spell. She said that back in her thick-walled ranch house around this time of day, she'd been in the habit of stripping down totally to lie atop her bedding during the dry heat of *la siesta*.

He told her to go ahead, adding, "It's too blamed hot for a member of the opposite gender to notice. Or leastwise, to *do* anything about anything he might notice."

She laughed roguishly and said she was tempted to just go ahead and test his self-control. She added it would certainly feel better, no matter what he thought about ladies cooling off as best they knew how.

He went on eating beans and cactus cross-legged as he told her to try and get some damned sleep, in any state of dress, while he stood guard. "I'll wake you up in time for you to spell me on guard for an hour or so. Then we'll be pushing those ponies, and ourselves, as if our lives depended on reaching the coast by morning, because they likely will."

She repressed a shudder, asked if he was trying to cool

her off by chilling her blood, and then calmly slipped her thin white dress off over her auburn head and lay back on the cotton flannel to close her big blue eyes with an innocent Mona Lisa smile. He couldn't help but notice she had auburn hair all over.

Her nipples were pink, and standing at attention on her small but nicely molded breasts. Her pale skin and slender build were surely new wonders to admire after his recent adventures with Rosalinda and Ampollita. But he looked away, lit a cheroot, and got up to stand guard on the far side of the tethered stock.

Of course, a man had to move about his post to cover all sides as he guarded it. So he naturally just had to catch a glimpse of her pale nude form from time to time, and then time again.

He had to laugh at himself for peeking. He muttered, "She knew you were close enough to just spread her thighs and enjoy as close a look as you wanted, if it hadn't been so hot and in such a dumb time and place. Haven't you figured her yet as what her own kind calls one of them *chifladas*? She wouldn't go on and on about it if she really *wanted* it. Did Rosalinda? Did Ampollita? Did any gal back home who wasn't a total prick-teaser? How many times have you told a pal not to waste his time and tips on a barmaid that swaps dirty talk with the boys bellied up to her bar?"

He took another drag on his cheroot and snorted, "Shit, even if it wasn't true, trying to lay anything that nice in this heat would kill you dead as those four Yaqui!"

Chapter 10

As anyone who studies deserts knows, the hottest days are usually followed by the coldest nights, since air baked dry can't hold much heat after sundown. Yet the night stayed balmy as the two of them rode the four ponies across trackless caliche at a pace that would have done the U.S. Cav proud. So Longarm wasn't surprised to glimpse distant flashes along the southern horizon, or wonder why the desert breezes from that same direction were commencing to taste more like seaweed than greasewood. When Consuela allowed they seemed to be in for another gully-washer, Longarm said, "I sure hope so. A good rain ought to erase our trail. But just in case it don't, let's ride."

They did, risking their mounts and their own necks on the thin edge of desperate. Mounted astride like a man with her feet braced in stirrups and her skirts hoisted scandalously, Consuela was a good rider. He knew she'd had more than livery stable experience when she didn't question his frequent trail breaks and changes of mounts. Longarm kept the four-mile-an-hour average of a good infantry column in mind as he rested the ponies more often and trotted them a mite faster.

So by first light, a tad after five in the morning because

of an overcast, they were wending their way downgrade through an ancient and wildly eroded lava field when suddenly, off to the southwest, they could see a real silvery sea and Longarm said, "We made it. Can't be more than a dozen miles from the coastline and it's downhill all the way."

Then fat raindrops landed all around to make cowpats of mud in the powdery dust. You didn't get caliche in a lava field. The chemistry was different as time and occasional but patient rainwater broke basaltic lava down.

Consuela sobbed, "We're going to get soaked! What will people say if I ride into town with my nipples showing through a thin wet dress?"

Longarm replied, "They'll say you've got great nipples. But hold the thought and let's swing closer to yonder wall of black rimrock. We may be able to find some shelter from the coming storm."

In such tricky light, it wasn't as easy as it sounded, but they did—by the time they'd gotten good and wet. The cavelike mouth of a lava tube, paved with a flat bottom of black sand, gave them more room than they and any number of scorpions and bats might ever ask for. Dismounting, they led the ponies in under the overhang. Longarm handed Consuela some of his wax matches to explore deeper as he broke out the best canvas tarp they had and stepped out into the rain with it to spread it flat in the downpour.

It poured down on him too. But he was already wet, so what the hell. He moved back inside to spy an orange glow, and following it around a bend in the glass-walled lava tube, found Consuela had built a small but cheerful fire, using windblown tinder and some dry sticks she'd found back there.

Longarm didn't ask why she was kneeling stark naked on a damp cotton flannel blanket. He glanced up at the shiny black ceiling and decided they could risk that much smoke for now. He knew her small blaze would die down

112

to smokeless coals by the time it got light enough outside to matter.

He nodded down at her and murmured, "*Tiene razon*, I'll fetch the saddles and we can drape stuff over the trees to dry some whilst we wait out this storm. You sure have tedious wet spells in this desert, no offense."

He leaned the Big Fifty against the black bumpy glass and moved to shift the damp saddles and such back to the small fire. Then he picked up their water bags and headed back to the mouth of the tube.

Once there, he placed his hat and the Schofield on a fallen black slab, sat down to haul off his boots, then stripped naked before he picked up the bags and stepped out into the deluge.

It felt swell.

The tempest from the muggy Sea of Cortez still held a hint of the tropical clime it had come from, and had he only had a bar of naphtha soap he'd have thought he was taking a shower after a long night in the saddle. But he didn't. So he was shaking out the now-clean tarp when Consuela, who somehow looked more naked, joined him there in the wet warm dawn to ask what they were doing.

Longarm sighed and said, "I was fixing to refill our water bags with the real stuff. I figured I could drape this tarp on the rocks so's to funnel rainwater into the bags. I mean to dump what the poor ponies have left of their cactus juice first and . . . Miss Consuela, would you mind going back inside with that teasing torso? I'm trying to get some *work* done here, and to tell the truth, I find naked ladies sort of distracting."

She laughed wickedly, reached down to grasp his semi-erection, and chortled, "So I see! Who said I was teasing?"

Then, as he really rose to the occasion, she gulped and added, "*Ay, que grande!* There seems to be more to you than meets the eye, and perhaps we should reconsider!"

So Longarm tossed the wet tarp on the gritty black sand,

took her chilled wet form in his arms, and proceeded to lower the two of them to the tarp as she gasped, "*No, esparte. Todavia es temprano*, and I did not expect you to take me this seriously!"

Then Longarm had her spread-eagle on the tarp, and his old organ-grinder hardly needed guidance as it parted the wet hair between her rain-slicked thighs and suddenly thrust, cold and stiff, into soft warm tightness as she stiffened in protest, sobbed, and then thrust upward with her firm young pelvis, pleading, "*Ay, estoy embrujada!* I cannot believe I am taking such a big gringo's *pipi* in my only-human *crica* and, oh, Custis! *Chinge me! Chinge me mucho!*"

So he did, and they both agreed it felt swell to let themselves go at it hammer and tongs in the warm summer rain like a pair of frogs mating in a lily pond, only better. He reminded her that frogs didn't get to stick it in, and she agreed the poor slithering things had to be missing a lot for all their croaking and splashing.

They tried it dog style in the rain, and managed to come that way as well, but then Consuela said she was getting chilled from all that rain on her back and running down between them. So they went inside and dried off to do it another way on a blanket by the fire. They agreed it was like starting all over with somebody new, save for the sweet fact you didn't have to mess around as much before you got started. She said she'd always found getting started sort of awkward, and he said he'd noticed. That made her laugh, accuse him of rape, and thank him for being so understanding by getting on top.

So, with one swell position and another, it was broad day outside by the time both the rain and their passions let up for the moment.

Not knowing what the sky had in store for the rest of the day, they got dressed, polished off the last of the beans and tomato preserves, and saddled up to ride on.

Patches of jagged-ass rock extended all the way down to the seacoast, Puerto Peñasco meaning about the same as Rockport, but they rode through a mile or more of cactus-hedged *milpas* of beans and corn before they drifted into the outskirts of the seaport via a farm lane instead of that coach road.

So not too many local folks seemed to pay them much mind, and she seemed pleased as punch by that. She said she had business that could wait, her southbound steamer not being due for a few days, and asked if they could find some out-of-the-way *posada* where her sordid but enchanting affair might not attract as much attention.

That was what some gals who just wouldn't leave a man alone called the inevitable results, a sordid but enchanting affair. She seemed to have herself convinced he'd seduced her with some Casanova spell. It allowed her to act wild as hell, though. So he had no call to argue.

He wasn't sure how much a man with a Mexican bounty posted on him ought to tell a gal of the currently ruling class down Mexico way. So he never did. He just said he was going out to see about innocent chores after they'd stopped at a dinky little inn near the waterfront. She said she'd let him, as soon as they tested the bedsprings just once. So seeing that he'd never had her in a real bed with a couple of pillows under her slim hips, they were going at it hot and heavy on the top floor while a Puerto Peñasco lawman had a cup of coffee and some conversation with the innkeeper down in the kitchen.

Having been paid in advance, the heavy-lidded innkeeper didn't care one way or the other, and it showed, as he told the town law that the mysterious gringo who'd arrived that morning was still screwing the not-bad-looking but rather skinny *blanca* he'd arrived with.

The lawmen sipped thoughtfully and murmured, "The one they wired us about was said to be traveling alone, with two mules he stole from a *fonda* to the north."

115

The innkeeper shrugged and said, "They arrived on horseback. The four ponies are out back in the corral if you wish for to examine them. I can show you their *vaquero* saddles, if you like."

The portly lawman shook his head and said, "Our country is so far from God and so close to Los Estados Unidos. There are gringos all over the place, and the one I seek crossed the border alone with one mule and one sorrel mare. After he had worn them out he stole two fresh mules. Nobody has reported any missing ponies. The couple upstairs may be just what they seem, a *chingado gringo* and a *puta* with poor taste in lovers. I shall keep an eye on them. But I do not see how either could be the notorious El Brazo Largo."

The innkeeper made the sign of the cross and gasped, "*Dios mio!* Is that who you thought I had upstairs, trying for to break my bedsprings with that bag of bones?"

The Mexican lawman sighed and replied, "If only that were so. Is a handsome reward being offered for the head of El Brazo Largo. Some business about him siding with rebels against our beloved El Presidénte. But the *malvado* they seek could hardly be down this way for to just get laid. So as long as that is all the one upstairs seems interested in, I shall only, as I said, keep an eye on him."

He finished his cup and left while, blissfully ignorant upstairs, Longarm was washing up at a corner stand, anxious to get going while the naked lady he'd just withdrawn from lay slugabed with her eyes closed, a dreamy smile on her lips as she spread her lean thighs wide to cool things off for a spell.

Slipping out of their room and down the back stairs, Longarm went first to the docks, asked directions, and found his way to the steamboat office.

He bought himself passage to Yuma, at the north end of their line. They told him the northbound would get in late that afternoon, be in port perhaps four hours, and shove off

116

for the night run north around ten P.M. That gave him more than enough time to sell those four ponies, buy himself another double-action .44-40 with a decent gun rig, take Consuela to supper after another good screwing, explain how he just couldn't stay, and still have time to slip aboard that coastal steamer before Harmony Drake and his own pals were likely to make a last-minute run for the gang-plank!

The sale of the ponies went off without a hitch, at a handsome profit, as soon as one considered how much he'd paid for them. The innkeeper, who seemed sort of anxious about something, helped Longarm out by telling him who to see about the deal.

He didn't have to herd four ponies anywhere. The Mexican horse trader came over late that morning to look the four brutes over, then dicker a bit before they shook on a price they both knew to be fair, and that was that. The innkeeper witnessed the sale, and the horse trader said he'd send his hired help over for the stock and the saddles after *la siesta*.

That just gave Longarm time to arm himself more sensibly, now that he was getting to be so rich off Mexican outlaws and Indians. So he asked directions and, packing the Big Fifty, with the Schofield tucked in his pants, headed for the gunsmith both the innkeeper and the honest horse trader recommended.

He was almost there, with the sun getting higher and hotter, when he spied a pair of ponies tethered in the shade of a cantina awning.

They were both saddled Anglo-style, which might not have meant as much if one hadn't been favoring its near hind hoof, having missed a shoe for many a weary mile. Longarm shut one eye to let its pupil adjust to dimmer lighting as he crossed the *calle* to stride on into the cantina with an innocent expression.

There were only two obvious Anglo riders in the nearly

deserted establishment. The older and shorter one sat in one corner behind a limed oak table with his back to the angled 'dobe. The one at the bar, as if to order, was tall and lean, packing a mighty familiar .44-40 in a cross-draw rig Longarm recalled having bought and paid for.

The one in the corner was staring out from under his Texas hat in such a disinterested way he just had to be interested as Longarm bore down on the one at the bar. That one didn't seem to notice Longarm approaching with the Schofield in his right fist and a cocked buffalo gun in the other. The *mestizo* barkeep cocked a brow and said something about opening another bottle as he headed on back to somewhere less tense.

The one packing Longarm's side arm, and doubtless a lot of other of his belongings, swung to face the man he'd robbed as he sensed an ominous movement to to his right.

There was no more delicate way to start. So Longarm strode closer to that one, a gun in either hand, and quietly said, "Howdy. Before you get your bowels in an uproar, I was only sent to bring in Harmony Drake. Would you rather fight another man's fight or make a deal?"

The kid wearing Longarm's gun blustered, "How would you like to try for a flying fuck at a rolling doughnut, Longarm? You ain't got any jurisdiction down this way and, come to study on it, I could give a little whistle and have you gunned down like a dog by them *rurales*."

Longarm quietly raised the Schofield, murmuring, "Do us both a favor and leave them sweet lips unpuckered. I don't think you follow my drift, old son. I'm offering you a break you never offered me the other night in Growler Wash. You'd be well advised to take it!"

The one in the far corner, who must have thought Longarm didn't know they were together, suddenly tipped his thick oak table forward and dropped behind it to make mysterious movements of his own. Longarm doubted he was jerking off. So before the Anglo could get his own gun muzzle over the top edge of his improvised barricade, Longarm swung the muzzle of the Big Fifty up to fire a shot heard all across Puerto Peñasco.

The cuss who'd made such an unwise decision squealed like a stuck hog for a short spell as he writhed in the corner on one side, with a belly full of oak slivers and distorted lead. As his agonized pissing and moaning subsided, Longarm quietly informed the other one, "I said I was willing to deal. I never said I was willing to put up with any more of this bullshit."

The younger and taller outlaw had gone fish-belly white and one got the impression, from the way both his hands were trembling at shoulder height, he was beginning to review his options seriously.

Then a voice from the doorway was saying in passable English, "I am not pointing my own guns your way for to ask your opinions of them, *caballeros*. You will both stand most still while my deputies put your weapons and everything else on the bar for my inspection. I am called Inspector Gomez, by the way. The words are the same in Spanish as English."

Longarm didn't turn as another Mexican in a gray summer uniform moved in to take both guns while a third searched him and put all his pocket jingle and his steamline ticket beside them on the bar.

The gun waddie he'd been fixing to relieve of far more suddenly blurted out, "He just killed my pard! You'll find the dead body over in yonder corner. He come in here, raving like a maniac, and just blew poor old Jake away."

Inspector Gomez, a stocky Mexican of about forty, moved over to the corner, took one look, and softly said, "I *thought* that was a buffalo round I heard from over in the marketplace. Your innocent friend seems to have a Remington .45 on the bloody floor by his right hand, señor. Could I have some names now?"

The snot who'd just surrendered Longarm's gun and

such to the Mexican lawmen smiled at Longarm as he said, "I'd be Sam Ferris, as innocent a child as ever rode out of Texas. Me and my poor pal, Jake Larkin, come down here looking to buy some of your fine dally-ponies. This murderous bounty hunter who just kilt Jake must have taken us for somebody else. He'd be that famous Longarm I understand your boys have had their own troubles with!"

Gomez turned to Longarm with renewed interest. "You are El Brazo Largo? For why were you registered at your *posada* as Señor Crawford?"

Longarm didn't like to lie when he didn't have to. So he simply smiled at Ferris and replied, "Ask him. *I* ain't the one packing the cross-draw .44-40 everyone says El Brazo Largo shoots *rurales* with."

Gomez swung about to stare thoughtfully at the gun rig his deputy had taken from Ferris to place atop the bar next to the Schofield .45 the real Longarm had been carrying. The burly Mexican lawman shoved Ferris back a pace to pick up the wallet they'd just taken from him. Ferris smiled weakly and said, "That ain't mine. We took it from *him*, see?"

Gomez opened the wallet to stare down at Longarm's federal badge and identification with a wolfish smile as he softly marveled, "You made Señor Crawford hand this over as he was covering you with a loaded revolver? I mean no disrespect, El Brazo Largo, but you seem to be trying to feed me a big bowl of *mierditas*! They say El Brazo Largo is a tall gringo who wears his .44-40 cross-draw. You are a tall gringo. You were wearing that .44-40 cross-draw, and you would seem to have had El Brazo Largo's badge and identification in your pocket. Would you care to explain how this might indicate this other noisy gringo, and not yourself, could be El Brazo Largo?"

Ferris nodded desperately and said, "Sure I can. I may as well confess me and poor old Jake were wanted over in San Antone, but not here in Mexico. We all know Longarm here is a lawman north of the border who's the wanted outlaw down *this* way. He chased us all this way illegal because he's after a pal of ours and—"

Gomezo cut in. "You say you were wanted by the *state* of Texas and so a *federal* deputy marshal tracked you all this way for to kill your friend with these antique weapons? Is that for why he registered at a second-rate *posada* with a woman and took his time for to encounter you by chance in this cantina?"

Ferris insisted, "It's true! He's Longarm, or El Brazo Largo as you all call him! We got the jump on him the other night, up the other side of the border. I took his gun rig because I fancied it. I've been packing his badge and identification because I meant to turn it in for the reward as soon as someone else I know finished his business here in Puerto Peñasco, see?"

Gomez turned back to the real Longarm, who shrugged and said, "Don't ask *me* why they'd get the drop on a famous lawman and forget to kill him before they rode off with his badge and gun."

Gomez softly said, "*Guns.* Plural. Did you not notice the derringer attached to that watch chain on the bar, Señor Crawford?"

Longarm shrugged again and said, "I stand corrected. Why don't we get him to tell us where this mysterious pal of his might be at the moment? Seems to me I'd want anyone who knew me to identify me if I was being confounded with somebody wanted by the local law. I'm pretty sure there's a lady back at my *posada* who can tell you I answer to the name of Crawford."

It didn't work. The portly Inspector Gomez smiled thinly as he shook his head and then said, "I have a better idea. I think I shall run you both over to *la cárcel* for to wait until we hear from higher authorities. We shall take photographs of the two of you and try for to make you comfortable in our most modern cells until it is decided who is to go free and who is to be shot, eh?''

Ferris protested he didn't want his pals to leave town without him.

Longarm said, ''For once I agree with this son of a bitch! I got me a steamboat to catch this evening!''

But Gomez just smiled and said, ''I noticed the ticket. If you are really who you say you are, it will still be good for passage to Yuma when we let you go. If you are El Brazo Largo, you will not be going anywhere but up against the wall, *comprende*?''

Chapter 11

When Inspector Gomez had bragged about the local jail being so modern, he'd meant the original oaken doors of the stone-walled cells had been replaced by iron bars, painted blood red. Prisoners still got to sleep on a floor mat and relieve themselves in a honey bucket. Their captors had prudently placed Longarm and Sam Ferris side by side in adjoining cells, separated by a thick slab of basaltic masonry. From their side of the bars, neither could see the modern Bell Telephone speaker that dangled between cells at face level.

But Longarm knew that old bromide about walls having ears had been inspired by ploys of the Spanish Inquisition. So when Ferris moved to the front of his own cell and called to him as "Longarm," the tall prisoner who'd given his name as Crawford repeated his alias as he ambled over, asking in a sincerely puzzled tone, "Who might you be performing for, old son? It's siesta time and I doubt that guard with his head on the desk out front speaks English, whether he's awake or not."

The outlaw picked up with Longarm's badge and gun insisted, "Come on, you know what I'm talking about, Longarm. They took both of our pictures in the office. It'll only take a few days for the Mex mails to put that fat greaser straight, and *then* where will you be?''

"Likely free as a bird, Longarm,'' the real Longarm declared with as happy-go-lucky a tone as he could muster. It would have been sort of dumb to say anything else, whether the walls were listening or not.

As if he could read minds, Ferris said, "All right. I don't owe *you* any favors neither. But I'd like to get out of here long before those photographs convince everyone you're a big fibber. So what if we let one hand wash the other? I might be able to get you out of here alive if you saw fit to spring me early.''

Choosing his words carefully, Longarm asked, "How do you figure I can get you out of here early, Longarm? You may not be able to tell from where you're standing, but this cell door seems locked secure and I just can't seem to reach that key ring on the desk out front without stretching considerably.''

Ferris said, "You could confess to being who we both know you are. They ain't going to let you go in any case. But if you told 'em I was me instead of you, they'd turn me loose and then I could see if I could get you out on one of them writs of habitual corpses, see?''

Longarm laughed for real, and declared, "You're all heart. First you accuse me of being a lawman who shot your pal, and now you want to bail me out? I heard about you during a similar stay in the Yuma jail, Longarm. They said you could lie like a rug and talk the horns off a billy goat. But I have to allow I expected you to be more good looking.''

Ferris swore and almost sobbed, "Lying to *me* ain't going to help you, Longarm. Look at my offer another way. Even if you figure it's a mighty slim chance, at least it's a *chance*. The greasers ain't fixing to offer you shit. You heard what that slob Gomez said about shoving the famous Longarm up against the nearest wall.''

The famous Longarm shrugged and replied, "I heard. I can see why you're so anxious about getting out of here before they can pin you down for certain. Old Gomez could have acted meaner. He let us both hang on to our smokes and matches. He didn't stick hot irons up your ass or mine. I thought that was pretty slick of him to have us both pose for our portraits instead. The trouble with beating answers out of prisoners is that they tell you what they think you want to hear instead of the truth. Is that why you keep trying to get out of this bind by accusing me of being you, Longarm? What if you were to own up to your own badge and identification so's *I* could see about getting *you* out?"

Ferris snorted in disbelief, and told Longarm to try something that was not only a physical impossibility but mighty undignified.

Longarm persisted. "You were the one who mentioned contacting a local lawyer and all. If you have pals here in Puerto Peñasco, I'd be proud to look them up for you."

Ferris snorted, "I'll bet you would. I saw what you did to old Jake with that buffalo gun. So all in all, I'd as soon give any pal of mine the galloping clap than an introduction to you!"

One story above them, Inspector Gomez removed the Bell receiver from his ear and wiped his face with a kerchief as he sighed, "*One* of them would seem to be *on* to us. Is a waste of time in this heat for to listen in on such guarded fencing with words."

He nodded at the worried-looking woman with auburn hair his men had brought from that *posada*. Consuela O'Hara y Mendez was guarding her own words as well. She had no idea what was going on, but as a woman of means on the run from a wayward husband, she sensed this was no time to confuse Inspector Gomez with her Father Confessor.

Gomez nodded to her pleasantly and said, "We are satisfied you are who you say you are, señora. Both your banker and the lawyer you named before as references have vouched for you and your family. I believe you when you say you and your, ah, associate down in the cell block met along the post road and arrived here after exciting but hardly unlawful adventures. I am sorry about the uncle you lost, killed by rebels against our beloved Presidénte. But is it not possible this gringo you know as Crawford was lying to you?''

Consuela had no trouble sounding sincere as she replied in a poised tone, ''For what reason? From the two photographs you just showed me, I can say the nicer-looking of the two men you hold identified himself to me as a Señor Crawford. And he got me out of the desert alive, after I had been abandoned to the mercy of heat, thirst, and Yaqui!''

''I said I believed all that,'' Gomez told her. There was no way a man with a political appointment could ask a young woman of good family and sensitive political connections whether she'd been serviced in any other way by a handsome gringo. So Gomez quietly asked, ''Did not your fellow adventurer give you any *first* name as the two of you rode all those miles together?''

Consuela naturally recalled Longarm's slip. She had no way of knowing it *had* been a slip. But she'd learned in her short adventurous life that men with oily smiles were seldom out to do her any favors, and Custis had been a dear about letting her get on top when she'd found his weight a bit too much for her on firm soil. So she shrugged and replied, ''I do believe he gave his full name when we first introduced ourselves. I've been trying to recall it. It may come to me later. I have never been able to tell Tom or Dick from Harry. All their names sound much the same to me.''

Gomez nodded gravely and said, ''I shall have two of my officers escort you back to that *posada,* señora.''

But Consuela shook her head as she rose, saying, ''I do

126

not intend to go back there. As I told you before, we rode in off the desert too tired to seek more proper shelter for our animals and ourselves. Now that I have had time to bathe and dress more properly . . .''

"I understand," Gomez said, adding, "In that case my officer shall escort you anywhere you *wish* for to go, señora."

As the man led her out of the room, Gomez turned to an older associate to place a finger alongside his nose and confide, "He meant less to her than he might have thought. We know more about her than I was ready to admit just now. She used the big tough gringo for to help her get safely away from a worthless husband. Whether he did anything more for her is unimportant. Any man alone with such a dish would wish for to taste some of it. The question is not what the one who calls himself Crawford has done to a lovely woman. It is who he really might *be*!"

His aide opined, "I find it hard to believe a woman of good family would lie for a wanted man unless she was most fond of him, Inspector."

Gomez nodded and replied, "I just said that. I told her we would let one of them go, as soon as we discovered which was El Brazo Largo. So why did she not ask when that might be if she had any intention of waiting for either?"

The aide agreed as, down on the *calle*, Consuela was getting into a carriage with two officers and a Mona Lisa smile. Was it *possible* she had actually made love, in the French manner, to a notorious as well as handsome wanted man?

Such an affair would be madness to carry on, of course, but her Custis had saved her life and been a great lay, and she could hardly wait to tell the other girls back home once she got her adventurous *culo* that far from Carlos and his own friends!

• • • •

As Inspector Gomez stared wistfully after her from an up-stairs window, his aide quietly called out, "They are talking again down below. Each is still insisting the other is El Brazo Largo."

Gomez yawned and decided, "Why do things the tire-some way when there is the easy way? Is impossible to guess which of them is the real thing or a most determined liar. But we shall have the straight answer soon enough from *rurale* headquarters. I am already late for my siesta. I suggest you take your own."

As the aide rose from the listening post, he asked if Gomez wanted anyone to listen in during the coming dark-ness, observing, "Late at night, when one cannot sleep, one may be inclined to babble, no?"

Gomez said, "No. they are not comrades in arms or even strangers picked up at the same time. They are sworn en-emies we arrested as they were enjoying a personal war. But look upon the bright side. I doubt we have any possible fear of them trying to break out together, and should one try it on his own, the other would be likely to sound the alarm."

The aide said, "Nobody but El Brazo Largo for certain would have a serious motive for to take such a risk. The one who is truthful about being someone else already knows he is in no danger of being shot as a menace to Mexico!"

Gomez smiled thinly and said, "Let us not get over-sentimental. *All* such gringo gunfighters are a menace to Mexico. But let us see which one deserves the firing squad with full ceremony and which can simply be disposed of with a bullet in the head before we concern ourselves with such details, eh?"

The aide agreed, and the two of them went home to their individual siestas. The hot muggy afternoon crept by less enjoyably for Longarm and his fellow prisoner in the wa-terfront jail. Longarm was out of tobacco and hungry as a bitch wolf by the time they were served a sunset supper of tortillas and frijoles which, without salt or seasoning, could be said to taste like white blotting paper wrapped around red clay.

In the next cell over, Sam Ferris betrayed a certain lack of border lore by demanding, "Jesus H. Christ! Do they expect us to eat shit on unfried flapjacks?"

Longarm soothed, "Frijoles only look like shit. They're mushed up beans and it's them, not the tortillas, that get sort of fried in a pan. Are you trying to tell me El Brazo Largo's never eaten any Mexican food before?"

Ferris almost sobbed, "Aw, cut that out, Longarm. You know we took the stuff they got in yonder desk away from you the other night. I can see what you're trying to pull. But it ain't gonna work."

Longarm moved over to sit on his floor pallet with his back to the stone wall as he slowly ate his tasteless supper, savoring every bite to make it last as the sun went down outside to make his grim cell seem even spookier.

The only light after sunset came from a desk lamp a young kid had brought in and lit for their armed guard, a burly *mestizo* who'd brought some books to read and didn't seem sleepy at all.

Longarm didn't want to attract attention by pacing. He'd already been over every inch of his small simple cell with his thoughtful and experienced eyes. There seemed no way out, whether their night man watched like a hawk or wandered off somewhere to play with himself.

The walls were dense basalt set in cement mortar. The floors were solid concrete slabs. Both the wooden ceiling and tiny barred window were too high to get at with nothing to stand on, and even if there had been something to stand on, those ceiling beams and iron bars looked too solid to gnaw through with one's teeth in any reasonable time.

Longarm finished the last of his lousy supper, decided against breaking the earthenware cup or saucer to use as a sharp edge for as long as it would take that guard to throw down on him through the front bars, and contented himself with simply sitting there to softly croon:

Away to war, across the water,
For seven years of blood and slaughter.
When I returned, Dunbarton's daughter,
Though pledged to me, was wed away!

From the next cell, Ferris yelled at him to shut up. So Longarm laughed and, having found something to amuse himself, switched to:

As I sat on Riley's doorstep,
Listening to the tales of slaughter,
Came the thought into me mind,
Why not shag the Riley's daughter?

Ferris wailed, and the guard out front glanced up from the novel he was reading to grunt, *"Ay, cállate la trompa."*
Longarm replied, *"Cóme mierda,"* then sang on about the delights of Riley's daughter as raucously as possible on purpose.

But it didn't work. The guard must have had orders, or a thick skin, since neither advising him to eat shit nor the very vulgar song in English seemed to inspire him to suit actions to his muttered threats. He only laughed when Longarm switched to Spanish lyrics, promising to piss on the guard's father's grave as soon as his old whore of a mother could figure out which of her many customers he might have been.

There was a lot to be said for cussing in Spanish. Since it had few words that were dirty all by themselves, the language called for more personal suggestions. For example, "son of a bitch" lost a lot of its bite when simply translated as *"hijo de perra."* So *"hijo de puta"* or *"so*

130

of a whore'' came out about as nice along the border.

Most everyone you drank with was a *cabrone*. The secret of starting a fight down this way was to mention any woman of his family, however politely, that he'd never introduced you to.

Longarm considered asking their guard whether it was true his sister was so fond of her burro because its dong was so much bigger than his own. But he decided against it. The cuss looked too smart to open the cell door without orders, and too Mexican to stand still for many serious insults without at least shooting somebody in the knee.

Another million years went by as silence set in, save for the sound of a page turning now and again. A fair piece after sundown, Longarm glanced up from his study of the dusty concrete floor as he heard their guard curse.

It took a few moments for Longarm to follow the devoted reader's drift. Then the lamp on the desk flickered again. Their guard put down his book and picked up the lamp to shake it. Once he'd determined there was plenty of oil left, he fiddled with the wick while the glass chimney blackened with sooty smoke until suddenly, the whole place was plunged into total darkness.

Almost total, at any rate. Longarm couldn't see his hand before his face as somewhere somebody opened something, judging by the draft of air on Longarm's hands as they gripped the bars of his cell.

Their guard must have felt it as well. He called out, *''Que pasa?''* and might have demanded, *''Quien es?''* had not further remarks from him been cut off in the dark by what sounded like someone slicing through a cabbage, followed by a large dull thud.

A familiar male voice called out, ''El Brazo Largo?''

To which Longarm could only reply, *''Aqui.* I thought that sounded like someone's throat getting cut, El Gato. Get me out of here. I got a boat to catch!''

There came the jingle of a key ring, but no sound of

approaching steps. They didn't call the rather sinister young man a cat because he stomped about in the dark in his boots and spurs.

As his invisible rescuer smoothly slid the right key in the lock, Longarm didn't ask how El Gato could see what he was doing. El Gato couldn't understand why everyone else seemed to go blind after the sun went down. But he'd long since learned to take advantage of his freakish night vision.

As he unlocked Longarm's cell, El Gato asked what their plans for Sam Ferris might be. The story of their cantina fight was all over town by this time.

Longarm stepped out, saying, "Let me get back my badge, my guns, and such whilst I ponder the prick's fate."

El Gato said, "*Mierda,* is no time for to ponder anything. I have your gun belt here. Put it on as we leave the premises *muy pronto*! I can unlock this other cell or leave it the way it is. Which shall it be, El Brazo Largo?"

Longarm laughed and said, "They have *him* pegged as El Brazo Largo to begin with, and they ain't going to give toad squat *who* he is when they find that guard with his throat slashed."

Then he called in to Ferris, "Are you ready to aid and abet the U.S. Justice Department instead of Harmony Drake, El Brazo Largo?"

Ferris naturally answered, "You can't leave me here with that dead greaser. I'll be lucky if all they want to do is shoot me! But who's this Harmony Drake you keep asking me about?"

Longarm told El Gato, "*Vamanos.* I haven't time for games. I told you I got a boat to catch and I know who's likely to be aboard it!"

So they and some other unseen presences left by way of a side exit to move along a dark alley. There was just enough light from the overcast sky above them to make out moving shapes. The nearest one with the big sombrero had to be El Gato. The other four figures could have been male, female, or big black bears for all one could really tell. As they moved swiftly but silently through the maze of back alleyways, Longarm buckled on his familiar .44-40. Then El Gato handed him his wallet and badge, saying, "One of my own may find that Schofield better for to carry than a pepperbox. What of that monstrous buffalo rifle they took away from you? Can we have it?"

Longarm said, "Not just yet. My Winchester's all the way over in New Mexico Territory by this time, Lord willing and they ain't lost all my baggage on me. I hope your *muchachos* hung on to that ammunition as well"

El Gato sighed and replied, "Our disgusting government seems to buy only modern guns and ammunition. Hey, how did you like that trick with the guard's night light, eh?"

Longarm chuckled fondly and said, "Couldn't have done it better my ownself. That kid working around the jail was one of your own, right?"

El Gato said, "*Sí,* is easy to place your own people in positions a grand government *cabrone* would not even choose for a brother-in-law. You know what was in that lamp instead of whale oil?"

Longarm nodded and said, "Sure. Water, with just a film of lamp oil floating on top to feed the wick for the first few hours of the night."

El Gato grumbled, "*Coño,* you peeked."

Longarm said, "Never mind how you got me out. Let's just say I owe you for that and show me the way to the docks. For I'm turned around total and I have to get aboard that northbound steamboat *poco tiempo,* lest it leave for Yuma without me!"

El Gato suddenly pulled Longarm through a doorway into a much more brightly lit corridor. Longarm could see all of them were dressed in black charro outfits now. One of them was wearing that bandolier and packing the Big Fifty.

El Gato himself was an almost girlishly good-looking gent who moved in a disturbingly slinky way. The scion of a pure Castilian clan he preferred not to name, the young rebel leader would have had no trouble passing as a dapper Anglo in a different outfit. But he preferred to dress like a *vaquero* in mourning, with his black wool and leather trimmed in shiny ebony and black lace. The friendly eyes he saw so well with in the dark could have been brown, dark blue, or even purple as they shifted constantly in the tricky hall light.

When Longarm repeated his urgent need to catch that boat, El Gato said, "Is too late. The night boat for Yuma left some time ago. Let us hope Inspector Gomez thinks you caught it. In either case they are certain for to turn this poor town upside down in search of you!"

Longarm swore softly and asked where El Gato was taking him.

The rebel leader pointed at the stairway down at the far end as he explained. "Next door to the room in which our good Inspector Gomez is in the habit of taking his siestas with a woman of La Causa. Is the last place Inspector Gomez would expect to find you, no?"

Longarm laughed incredulously and demanded, "Jesus H. Christ, you expect me to hide out in a whorehouse?"

El Gato shrugged and replied, "Were you planning for to hide behind a cactus? Is no better cover for two days' ride in any direction!"

Chapter 12

They led the thoroughly battered Sam Ferris from his cell at dawn, then out of town a mile, where they made him dig his own grave by the side of the road. When Inspector Gomez finished his morning coffee, he rode out to join them.

Gomez smiled in a fatherly way and declared, "Everything you told our midnight shift would seem to hold together, gringo. Was three other men and one woman staying at that waterfront hotel you named. They left, as you said, on the night boat for Yuma. Perhaps they will get there. Perhaps not. I have wired *los rurales* at San Louis Rio Colorado, where their vessel must pass through customs before proceeding on up the delta into your own country. The descriptions you gave of your leader and two henchmen were not too helpful. But how many blondes pass through San Luis Rio Colorado in a given period, eh?"

Ferris failed to puff the lit cigarette a guard placed between his bruised lips. He pleaded, "I told you that was the real Longarm you had in the very next cell. So how come I'm standing here in this old hole?"

Gomez pleasantly replied, "Because you would stink terribly in this heat if we did not bury you. Tell me for why you and your band came all this way down from Arizona Territory if Arizona Territory was where you wished for to be.''

Ferris sobbed, ''I've told you over and over! We were holed up fine near Yuma when old Harmony went into town and got picked up by the law. Harmony was wanted on federal charges. So when we heard they was sending Longarm to transport him back to Denver, we had time to set up a trap. We knew Longarm was too good to die the way we left him. We *wanted* him to bust loose, flag down a train, and tell everyone we'd run off to Mexico, see?''

Gomez wrinkled his nose and asked, ''You really ran for where you wished him for to say you were running?''

Then, before Ferris could answer, the wily manhunter nodded as if to himself and said, ''That explains all those boat tickets. Your friends are doubling back to a hideout that would have been ideal if this Harmony Drake had only behaved himself. No Yanqui lawman knows of it to this day. Or should I say no Yanqui lawmen *knew* of it until he tracked you this far? El Brazo Largo had booked passage aboard that same night boat before he somehow slit the throat of the desk sergeant from an impossible distance.''

Ferris cried, ''I told you some Mexicans came to bust him out. I can tell you where Harmony, Goldmine Gloria, and the boys are headed too!''

Gomez grimaced and coldly replied, ''Is not important to *me*. I know it was El Gato or some of his people who helped a known friend escape. I have no jurisdiction in Arizona Territory. I intend to catch the one I am really after on my own side of the border. Whether your friends go to Yuma or to Hell is of no interest to me.''

As he started to turn away, Ferris pleaded, ''What about me then? If you don't give a shit about anyone but Longarm, what am I standing in this hole for?''

Gomez shrugged and quietly replied, ''Is the best place for us to dispose of an unimportant stink. Is no reward posted for you on either side of the border, and you pests make so much noise at the Americano Consulate every time we bruise you just a little. So all in all, I feel this may be best for all concerned, eh?''

Then he said *"Ahora"* in a conversational tone, and turned to leave as they shot Ferris to a bloody mess in the bottom of his shallow grave.

Once he got back to his headquarters, Gomez wired San Luis Rio Colorado for further news on that night boat, and ordered his men to keep the pressure on in the unseemly parts of town, observing that lowlifes who were not being paid to hide wanted men were inclined to want them caught, if only so they could get back to their own shady business.

Then, after a tedious morning defending his country, the ponderous patriot enjoyed an early snack and waddled over to his favorite house of ill repute to enjoy a few hours of sensual siesta time.

As he was being serviced by a slender *mestiza* with hips that just kept moving and eyes that held no expression at all, the man he had his whole force searching for in *other* houses of ill repute was in the next room, pacing the floor and puffing furiously on the big *claro* cigar El Gato had brought him. The saturnine Mexican himself sat on the windowsill, idly staring down at the street through the slats of the blue pine shutters.

The walls of the solidly built *chincheria* were too thick for them to hear what Gomez was begging for next door. It was just as well for Gomez's peace of mind that he couldn't hear El Gato's answer when Longarm asked why they were letting the fat lawman live.

El Gato said, "Is a matter of the devil we know against a new one who might be better. Gomez is good, but not as good as he thinks he is. Nobody could be. His weakness is that when the *putas* tell him how much everybody fears him, he believes them. But about that government payroll shipment my friends and me are here for. Do you wish for to be in on it or not? Your share would be better than ten percent, if you could spare a few extra days down this way.''

Longarm didn't want anyone calling him a sissy. So he said he just loved to take part in payroll robberies as a rule, but had to get on down the road. When he asked again about any other boats headed north, El Gato said, ''Patience, my idealistic youth. I told you there were boats and then there were boats. Would be suicide for anyone on our side to put out to sea before sundown. This tiresome government we've been suffering under has bought a fleet of steam cutters from that old *cosita* Queen Victoria for to guard our coasts against piracy. That is what El Presidénte calls catching fish without paying him off: piracy.''

El Gato turned from the window, adding, ''The streets below are now clear of friend and foe. Is too hot outside for anyone. After the woman of La Causa has learned more from our gallant Gomez, we shall perhaps be able to plan your mad dash up the coast with more certainty, eh?''

Longarm smiled thinly and asked, ''Does Gomez always blab all his plans to the ladies?''

El Gato nodded soberly and explained, ''That is for why I asked them to give him a good price. When a man thinks he is getting it almost for nothing, he is inclined to think she must *like* him. Married men in the habit of patronizing *putas* are seldom simply oversexed. Women who make a business of pleasing men are inclined to let men talk, no matter how boring they may seem at home. I understand our gallant Gomez is saddled with a delicate faded rose who does not like for to hear about clever questioning or ingenious disposals, eh?''

Longarm said he followed El Gato's drift, then added, ''No matter where he thinks I ran to, I have to get going if I mean to catch up with Harmony Drake and his pals. I

I wait until dark, they'll have put in at Yuma long before I can hope to get there!''

El Gato shrugged and suggested, "Forget about them and help us steal money instead. Is no way you could overtake that night boat before it puts in at Yuma. Not if you left this very minute. I told you the only vessels our side controls are fishing boats or, all right, smugglers, powered by sails in the fickle winds of this stagnant Sea of Cortez. Your prisoner and his blond *puta* will be back on shore, free for to run in any direction, long before we could hope to land you in Yuma. To begin with, is a guarded border crossing you would never get through if you followed the main channel of the Rio Colorado. The broad swampy delta provides many better, or at least less famous channels. But progress through that windless sea of tule reeds can be slow."

"I don't aim to catch 'em aboard that infernal steamboat." Longarm declared, snorting smoke out both nostrils as he explained. "The best I can hope for in Yuma is somebody who saw which way they were headed. Such witnesses get tougher to come by as time winds on. They *know* this. They figure they led me on a long ride around Robin Hood's Barn, and I'm figuring they heard I'd been arrested before they ever boarded that side-wheeler. Even if they take some pains, it's tough to cover your tracks when you get off a steamboat with a good-looking blonde. I only need someone who can say for certain they caught a train either way. I'm betting they never planned to."

El Gato cocked a thoughtful eyebrow. *"Por que?* For why would anyone stay close to Yuma when he knew that was where the law expected them to hide out?"

"To hide out, of course," said Longarm, taking pity on his pal's bewildered smile. "Harmony Drake was the only member of the bunch anyone ever spotted in Yuma. Or should we say, the downtown parts of Yuma. I'm saying they must have been holed up somewhere good.

139

Somewhere they felt safer than anywhere here in Mexico where nobody in possession of a U.S. federal warrant had just cause to look for them.''

El Gato nodded soberly and said, "Is agreed those two you tangled with in that cantina should not have been out drinking when they had reason for to be expecting someone like you to come along. But should the gang leave that boat for to go straight to some Yuma hideout, do you have any idea where such a secret lair might be?''

To which Longarm could only reply, "Upstairs or down, close to the center or way out on the outskirts of town. A hideout is by definition somewhere nobody else knows about. With any luck, I'll be able to trace them as far as the depot, and we can wire an all-points on the sneaky sons of bitches. But with my luck, they'll go to ground somewhere close to Yuma, where Billy Vail sent me to get old Harmony in the first damned place. How long does it take a sailboat to carry a lawman that far, old son?''

El Gato said, "Twenty-four hours with a following wind. It gets to be more of a problem when the winds are calm or contrary. I think you have more fun helping us rob El Presidénte Diaz. They gonna kill you if they catch you anyway. So you may as well have the game as long as you have the name, no?''

Longarm grimaced and said, "It sure beats all how they ban books suggesting it feels good to get laid, whilst you'll find a copy of *Robin Hood* in most every school library. That one book has got more folks killed than all the French postcards ever printed. It ain't wise to tell little kids it's all right to commit highway robbery if you don't like the sheriff.''

El Gato shrugged and said, "I spit in the milk of your Robin Hood's mother. I fight for Mexico in the tradition of El Cid, the grandfather of all Spanish-speaking rebels. When *his* king shit on him, El Cid went loco and killed people until they apologized sincerely. But be off to Yuma in search of the goose if you must. I shall send word to our most sneaky smuggler, Dandolo. Nobody knows this rocky coast and the swampy Colorado Delta more better than Dandolo. But if she agrees for to take you up to Yuma, you must let her do it her own way and set her own pace, *comprende*?''

Longarm stopped pacing and frowned. "*She?* This Dandolo is a *gal*?''

El Gato nodded. "Did I not just say she was sneaky? I understand she is not even a true Mexicana. Her family came here from Venice years ago as coastal traders. Perhaps that is for why Dandolo speaks so many languages. Her crew more than makes up for any lack of brawn Dandolo has for to go with her brains. Her vessel, a Yanqui schooner she inherited from her father, is fast and, even better, shallow-draft. The delta of the Rio Colorado has always been tricky for to navigate, and they tell me that lately, since your Anglo settlers have been drawing irrigation water from its tributaries, it has gotten worse.''

Before Longarm had to say he was sorry about that, there came a soft tapping on the bolted oaken door. El Gato opened it to admit a pleasingly plump *puta* in a loosely fastened robe.

As El Gato closed and barred the door behind her, the gal told them, "The pig is asleep, filled with wine, empty of desire, and most pleased with himself. *Telegrafo* messages move faster than the winds. So Gomez knows a, how you say, squall line is moving up the coast. He says we are to get hit with much wind, rain, thunder, and lightning just after the sun goes down.''

Longarm cocked a brow. "You say this *pleases* Gomez?''

The whore who'd doubtless also pleased the inspector nodded and explained. "He says that if you were not aboard that night boat bound for Yuma, you must be hiding here in Puerto Peñasco and must be most anxious for to

141

leave before they can turn over the wet rock you must be hiding under. I mean no disrespect, El Brazo Largo. Was *him* who said this, not me."

Longarm nodded and told her to go on. So she continued. "Gomez expects you to make a break for it by sea during the coming storm. He has ordered the crew of that steam cutter at the far end of the embarcadero to stoke their boilers no later than three this afternoon, so they will have the full head of steam before sundown. When I yawned in his face and played with his *pipi,* he naturally thought I did not find his plans so interesting. So he naturally insisted on telling me how that cutter would find itself out on a calm sea in the moonlight if it cast off in the teeth of that squall as it swept north."

Longarm and El Gato exchanged thoughtful glances. El Gato sighed and said, "I must learn not to underestimate the sly *fregado*. They have a Gatling gun mounted on that cutter, and is no way Dandolo can outdistance it by sail alone under a full moon!"

Longarm said, "I know. Is it right to picture this government cutter something like a big single-masted sloop, rigged fore and aft, with the mainsail set back a tad to make room for a steam funnel and that deck gun?"

El Gato nodded soberly. "Under sail or steam she is *muy pronto*. Is no paddle wheels. She has a modern screw propeller and one of those keels you can haul up for to tear across shallow water. They must have heard how certain people avoid the official entry port at San Luis Rio Colorado. In any event, is no way for you to leave by sea for at least a few nights."

Longarm took a thoughtful drag on the *claro* before he asked, "What if I left earlier? I told you I was in a hurry to get it on up to Yuma whilst the trail of those outlaws is still warm. And seeing they mean to get up a full head of steam *before* that gale hits at sundown, I have no call to let it go to waste, do I?"

The whore had no idea what he was talking about. El Gato laughed like a mean little kid, and told her she'd best get back to her fat customer.

As the rebel leader locked the door after her, he told Longarm, "Dandolo may be willing. She is almost as *loco en la cabeza* as yourself. I have yet to grasp why it should be so that people who are not true Mexicanos seem to enjoy our revolutions more than we do!"

Irena Dandolo soon arrived with some of her piratical-looking "fishermen." *She* looked like a pirate too.

The sun- and wind-tanned woman of perhaps thirty or so, give or take a rough life on the bounding main, was tall and wiry for a female but not bad looking, once you got used to the scar on her forehead and her short-cropped dark-brown hair. She was dressed in rope-soled *zapatas*, white bell-bottoms, and a striped Basque shirt that didn't really appear as manly as she might have wished. She had quite a pair of *chupas* for such a lean athletic figure.

She shook hands with a firm grip, and her palm felt as if she knew her ropes. Longarm admired the way she grinned when he told her his plan. He still felt obliged to say, "It's not really your fight and the odds favor the other side, Miss Irena."

The female skipper looked hurt and demanded, "Do you take me for a mere woman just because I *am* a woman? Listen, Yanqui, I am a direct descendant of Enrico Dandolo of Venice! You have heard of him, no?"

Longarm smiled sheepishly and asked, "Should I have?"

She snapped, "Of course. You English-speakers make so much of that boy-buggering *mariposa* Richard of England when it was the men and the ships of Venice who made all those crusades possible. My ancestor, Enrico Dandolo, led the ladder assault over the walls of Constantinople in 1204. This would not have been so remarkable in itself. He was from Venice, after all. But at the time he was in

143

his nineties, and *blind*! You think it would have slowed him down if he had been born with a slit between his legs?''

Longarm gulped and declared, "Not enough to matter, ma'am. But how come this blind old hero was attacking Constantinople during one of those crusades. Wasn't that a *Christian* town at the time?''

The ferocious old man's proud descendant sweetly explained that her ancestor had been blinded in a much earlier war with the Greeks of Constantinople, and added, "There were always *Moors* for to kill. When he saw the chance to kill some old *enemies,* it was too good for to pass up. He died just a year after he led the assault over the walls of Constantinople. He must have died content, after a life well spent. I would die with a smile upon *my* lips tonight if I knew I had done something to annoy a most annoying government!''

So later that afternoon, as the streets came back to life after *la siesta,* under an oddly greenish sky with the taste of brass in the muggy air, the engineer in the hold of *El Tiberon Blanco* valved a little pressure off as he eyed the gauges of their small but very up-to-date Scottish auxiliary plant. The iron-framed and teak-sheathed cutter was built for short, furious bursts of speed, while intended to cruise under sail as often as possible. She burned oil instead of coal, to keep her light and fast. But oil cost money and it was not to be wasted.

Up in the cockpit, aft the mainmast, under furled sails, the skipper and deck crew were keeping an eye on that discolored sky. It was intolerably hot and damp in port that afternoon, and they were all anxious to put out to sea, where the motion of their vessel alone might offer some cooling breeze. But orders were orders and they had to wait until that storm hit, or until they spied another vessel of any kind putting out to sea ahead of it.

For who but *ladrones* up to no good would be shoving

off this late in the day with storm warnings flying above the harbor master's watchtower?

Up forward, under the meager shade of the furled jib, the three-man crew of the swivel-mounted Gatling gun were swapping dirty stories as they casually eyed the crowd along the quay.

Nobody drifting in and out of the waterfront shops or simply staring at the boats looked sinister. But when one manned a Gatling for as popular a tyrant as Porfirio Diaz, one kept one eye on the taxpaying public at all times.

Hence it would have been tough to just swagger across the fifty feet of cobblestones from the nearest cover to come aboard the cutter via the one gangplank near the stern.

So just as the sun was setting, where the brassy-smelling sky met a bruised-looking sea of smooth but ominously large swells, considering the total lack of any breeze, Longarm nudged Irena Dandolo, who in turn gave the signal on her bosun's whistle.

That naturally alerted the government men aboard the cutter, just as Longarm had hoped. So the quay began to clear as if by magic when the deck crew swung the multiple muzzle of that Gatling shoreward, like a deadly pepper shaker sniffing for someone to pepper.

Longarm knew they couldn't see him as he raised the muzzle of the Big Fifty in the narrow slit between a ship's chandler and a sidewalk cantina. He drew a careful bead on the one aiming the Gatling and blew him over the low starboard rail with a well-aimed buffalo round.

That inspired two of his shipmates to dive over the far side as the others took cover below decks.

That had been the plan. Yelling like a band of Yaqui with toothaches, the eight men and one woman of the Dandolo crew charged across the open field of fire with Longarm, blazing away with carbines or six-guns as instructed, until they were all aboard with only one of their own lightly

145

wounded, mopping up with guns and machetes at close quarters.

The wounded survivors of the other side were allowed to live, as long as they knew how to swim, while *El Tiberon Blanco* cast off and steamed across the bar into the sunset, people shouting curses and encouragement from the bewildered shore.

The cutter was a distant dot against the sunset by the time a most chagrined Inspector Gomez climbed up into the harbor master's watchtower to make certain his second in command had not been drinking.

For quite some time Gomez could only rant and rave. Then he heaved a great sigh and decided, "We must wire San Luis Rio Grande and confess they shoved it up my ass while I was bending over. Is more important for to *stop* that double-thumbed son of a two-headed witch than it is for me to simply go on sounding smart. People such as El Brazo Largo are most *expensive* for to share this earth with. First he wipes out that artillery column in the Baja, and now he has stolen a brand-new steam cutter from us!"

Chapter 13

The groundswells rolling ahead of the oncoming storm had the stolen cutter bucking pretty good as Irena Dandolo took the helm, set a course with the brass binnacle ahead of the wheel, and called for her crew to set the jib and mainsails.

Longarm, clinging to a steel cable stay as he stood beside her in the cockpit, stared thoughtfully aft, where the twilight sky was swirling mighty strangely, and quietly observed, "That squall line we've been promised seems to be coming up the trail behind us, Miss Irena. I know I ain't no sailor. But is this really the time to be setting all those sails?"

The seawoman laughed girlishly and replied, "I wish for to give us a head start on any *marina federale* boats following us. I know more about sails than engines. Nobody in my crew knows much more. Is possible the machinery below will stall, or run out of fuel, before we make it to the reed beds of the Colorado Delta. Is better to be far from Puerto Peñasco than near it when that happens, eh?"

Longarm said he hoped she knew what she was doing. Then he went below via the hatch and ladder ahead of the cockpit to see if her crew could use someone who could at least read.

They could. In the dinky engine room just aft of the mainmast, he caught up with a Mexican and a Sandwich Islander, coping as best they could, by feeble lamplight, as the duckboards under them rocked like a corkscrew. The brass telegraph, in this case a signal device worked by push-rods rather than electricity, was set at full ahead, and the Islander, a big Kanaka who answered to Monakai, had that part figured out. He knew enough about steam engines to have the throttle valve wide open. When asked, neither allowed that the half-dozen dials set at eye level between the upright boiler and compact opposing cylinder engine meant anything to them.

Longarm left things the way they were for the time being as he studied the setup and tried to recall such steam lore as he knew. The vessel was bucking to one side now, and the screw made the hull hammer as if a Navaho way-chanter was beating it for a cure whenever the spinning blades broke the surface near the rudder. So Longarm got a grip on a grab-iron with one hand, and used the other to ease back on the throttle to cruising speed, which might have been six knots in a calmer sea with the screw in the water all the time.

The Mexican, called Bajo, or Shorty, despite his formidable size, quietly observed that Dandolo had signaled full speed ahead.

Longarm nodded agreeably and replied, "She just told *me* she was afraid we'd run out of fuel oil. You can hear for yourself how that screw's just churning through air half the time. May as well be using less steam up as we ride out this blow. Let's see if I can make any sense out of those dials now."

As he moved along the line of pipes and fittings, Bajo put a big greasy paw on his dirty shirtsleeve and growled, "Hey, gringo, *I* am in charge here."

Then Longarm twisted free to face them both, narrow-eyed but still smiling as he quietly said, "*No me jodas*. I mean that. There are times to fuck around and there are times the situation is just too serious for kid games.''

Bajo took a swing at him.

Longarm had figured he might. So his left forearm came up to block the roundhouse blow as his right hand whipped his .44-40 from its cross-draw rig. So Bajo was throwing a left hook as Longarm stepped inside the radius of his swing and cracked him across the mouth with the steel barrel.

That busted the bully's face up a lot, although Longarm had been careful not to break off any teeth this far out to sea. His aim was to set an example, not to saddle Irena Dandolo with a cripple in dire need of a dentist.

As Bajo cowered back against the engine room ladder, holding a hand to his shattered, bloody lips, Longarm mildly asked the somewhat taller Monakai whether he had any comment.

The big Kanaka shook his head and replied, "It's not my fight. I know better than to take a punch with a fist at a man who's wearing a gun!''

Bajo nodded and sobbed, "Was not fair for to use a gun on me when I only wished for to punch you a little!''

Longarm said, "I didn't *use* this gun on you, *pendejo*. I mean to the next time you start up with me. I told you not to fuck with me. That was one strike. You fucked with me and I busted your lip. That was two strikes. You fuck with me again and I'll strike you out for good!''

Then he put his gun back in its holster, adding, "*Bueno*. As I was saying when I was so rudely interrupted, we'd best see if we can nurse at least a hundred and fifty nautical miles out of this Scotch hardware.''

The water level in the boiler seemed high enough. Longarm took a pencil stub from his shirt pocket, wet the lead with his tongue, and marked the glass before he called the more sensible Kanaka over.

When Monakai proved willing to listen, Longarm

pointed to the mark and a valve just above it, saying, "We want water in this tube below that pencil mark and steam above it. I know it's moving up and down a mite. The rocking of the hull is sloshing the water in the boiler. The idea is not to flood the boiler until there's no room for the steam, but also not to let her boil so dry we could have us an explosion. The way you get a steam boiler to explode is to let it get so hot and dry a sudden surge of water against hot steel produces more steam, all at once, than the boiler plates or safety valve can cope with. So this tube and injection valve ought to be kept in mind."

The Kanaka said he followed Longarm's drift. Bajo moved away up the ladder, pissing and moaning about his fool face, as Longarm showed Monakai the reserve water gauge and explained how you had to inject cool fresh water, pumped by steam pressure, into the seawater-cooled condenser from time to time. For while in theory the steam went from the cylinders to the condenser to turn back into boiler water over and over, in practice you always lost some steam forever.

The Kanaka said Longarm was sure smart.

To which Longarm could only reply, "Not hardly. This fuel gauge is the snake in the grass I can only guess at. I have it on authority of the Union Pacific that you burn around five pounds of coal an hour for each and every horsepower of your steam engine. This here's a forty-horsepower engine. But it's burning *oil*, which weighs a quarter as much as coal for the same amount of heat. So let's see, a pint is a pound the world around, so a gallon of oil ought to give off the heat of sixty-four pounds of coal and . . . Kee-rist!"

The big Sandwich Islander swore as loud in his own odd lingo as gallons of seawater poured down the ladder to slosh ankle-deep or deeper across the duckboards. The dimly lit chamber filled with brine-scented mist as some seawater sloshed against the hot metal of the firebox, and

Monakai sobbed, "Tangaroa and Tiki Jesus, we are sinking!"

Longarm told him not to blubber up about it, and added, "We'd best go topside just in case you're right. I told that gal she was setting full sail at a mighty awkward time!"

Monakai wasn't listening. He was already halfway up the ladder.

Then all the water sloshed into one corner and stayed there as the hull stayed on her starboard side at an ominous angle. So Longarm set the throttle at dead slow and went topside after the big Kanaka.

He wasn't certain he should have, as his face got lashed and his duds got soaked through by horizontal wind and rain. He groped his way aft through the howling darkness to find Irena Dandolo singing, or screaming, at the wheel as she steered them over rolling ranges of foaming brine with one rail under. Longarm had to almost shove his nose up her ear for her to hear him as he shouted, "You're fixing to capsize us! You can't leave all your canvas up in a full gale!"

She cackled like a pretty witch jerking off with her broom and insisted, "Of course I can. You call this a gale? Wait until you ride out a hurricane with us! Foul weather is the friend of pirates and smugglers. We must be making eighteen knots in this squall, but alas, it is already letting up!"

Longarm shouted, "You call this a *letup*?" as green water came over the taffrail to soak them both to the thighs. But he had to allow they weren't heeled over quite as far now, and the wind had died from actually painful to just frightening.

Irena asked him why he'd throttled back the engine. He made note of the fact that she knew what she was doing after all, and told her, "We were wasting fuel stirring foam with the screw out of the water that often. I left her turning over fast enough to keep from dragging against the sails, and it's best to be using some steam with fire under the boiler than it is to let it just build up with nobody manning the relief valve.''

She swung the wheel to catch more wind as they crested a sea. Then she said, "Maybe I should sign you on as my engineer. For why did you break Bajo's face like so? Were you jealous? Listen, is not true I have been sleeping with Bajo. He just likes to talk. I never sleep with anyone who works for me. Is very bad for business for to do that. How do you fire a lazy worker after you have let him pick your flowers, eh?''

Longarm nodded gravely and allowed he followed her drift as she steered a course a New England skipper might have found too rich for his blood.

Longarm told her he'd pistol-whipped Bajo for getting in the way while he was trying to make sure they weren't fixing to blow up. He added, "It ain't that I'm an infernal steam engineer, Miss Irena. But I've seen a steam boiler blow a time or more and it ain't a pretty sight.''

She asked if he had any idea how much steam they could count on between where they were and the Colorado Delta.

He answered truthfully, "I can't say. If we can coax eight or ten miles an hour out of this tub, we ought to have enough. If we can't, we don't. Where were you figuring on refilling your fuel tanks, up Arizona way?''

She laughed and asked what made him think the storm-lashed cutter would be coming back from Arizona. Then they crested a whopper of a wave and the wind-filled sails laid *El Tiberon Blanco* on her beam ends.

Longarm was sure they were fixing to turn turtle. Someone else was too. For the vessel began to slowly right herself as the wild gal at the wheel shouted, "*Condenado!* Who reefed the mainsail without my *permiso*?''

Longarm could just make out the bare mast whipping back and forth against the rain-lashed overcast as the big Sandwich Islander, Monakai, joined them in the half-flooded cockpit to shout, above the gale-force wind, "You were driving her under! The hero Maui with all his *mana* could not ride out a blow like this with two hulls if he had those damned sails set!"

Irena yelled, "*Eso es una mierda!* I know what I am doing, and I ought to send you back to your cannibal island for to be sucking on your mother's *chupa* like the big baby you are!"

Before the impassive Kanaka could answer, the wind died as if some monstrous door had slammed shut in the sky behind them, and while the waves rolled on as high, the surface was now smooth and black as India ink.

Then the full moon was smiling down on them through the thinning cloud cover, and Irena laughed and said, "Our Inspector Gomez knew what he was talking about. If we had survived that squall line in our smaller schooner, this bigger tub and its Gatling would be leaving port at this moment for to hunt us down as we sat becalmed with no engine! Take the helm, Monakai. El Brazo Largo and I must go below and see how far we can push this hull with no help from the wind!"

She didn't have to tell Longarm to follow her. He wanted to know as much as she did. Down in the engine room the water they'd taken through the hatch had drained away into the bilge, but the lamp had gone out and the only light came from the blue flames of the firebox under the boiler. It worked something like a glorified oil stove. An inventor back East had patented an air-blower to fan such flames far hotter. But the notion hadn't caught on as yet. Modern machinery was complicated enough without having to gussy it up with fancier gingerbread.

As Longarm relit the lamp, he asked what she'd meant about having no serious plans about a return trip. He asked if she and her crew planned on settling down north of the border.

She shook her curly head and replied, "Someday, after

we rid poor Mexico of that *Chingado* Diaz, I may be the first woman admiral of the *marina federale*. El Gato told me you were most serious about the laws of your own country and that I should not let you catch me breaking any Yanqui laws before I got you *locura de amor*. I fear I do not see why this should be so. To betray a lover for La Causa is considered *muy romantico* where I come from."

Longarm laughed as he got out his notebook and pencil stub to calculate their fuel reserves, observing, "It's my own fault I told El Gato that much about our courts of law as we were killing a long night around a campfire. That boy sure has a wicked sense of humor. He thought it was mighty funny that I wasn't supposed to mess with a female suspect, lest her lawyer use that against us at her trial."

He jotted down some dial figures, calculated roughly, and assured her there was no way in hell they were ever going to steam all that way north to Yuma. Then he said, "I figure you got enough oil to carry us a tad over a hundred miles, depending on how you nurse your steam. So that leaves us forty to sixty miles short of the mouth of the Colorado, and Gomez will have wired San Luis Rio Colorado that we're on our way."

Irena shoved the throttle to full speed ahead and said, "We shall put some distance between ourselves and anybody a *puerco* called Gomez may send after us. By morning there will be a fair sea breeze as the inland desert heats up for to suck. We shall *sail* the sixty miles our fuel tanks lack. That should leave us the reserves we need for to play tag among the tules of the delta with anyone trying for to cut us off. How does an American go about getting out of your prisons by saying somebody screwed her with a badge, eh?"

Longarm put his notebook away with a weary smile, saying, "I never treat friend or foe that way with my badge, Miss Irena. Even if I did, it wouldn't get anybody out of prison. It would only make it a mite tougher for me to *pu*

154

'em there. Judges and juries frown upon the arresting officers taking advantage of prisoner gals, or using what they say in bed as evidence.''

She said she wasn't sure what he meant. So he told her to just not tell him about anything crooked she was planning for north of the border.

She sighed, reached up to trim the lamp, and as the engine room was plunged into a romantic darkness, save for the faint blue glow from under the boiler, leaned against Longarm with her arms around his damp shirt and husked, *"Bese me con ferocidad* and do not ask about any other sins I may have in mind then!''

Longarm kissed her. It seemed only polite. Then it felt swell. But he had to question her common sense, if not her motives, when she reached down between them to unbutton his fly and reach inside his pants for what was only acting natural.

As her rope-calloused hand grasped his turgid organ-grinder, he removed his lips from hers long enough to quietly ask if she'd lost track of where they were at the moment.

She squeezed harder and softly replied, ''I bolted the door after us as we came down the ladder. Would make my crew feel left out if I took you to the cabin I have claimed from *los federales*. Better we rage together down here, no?''

Longarm winced and pleaded, ''Not so hard. My poor old ring-dang-doo is only flesh and bone right now. I follow your drift about your cabin, but that floor underfoot is not only wet but duckboarded. I wouldn't want your own fair flesh bruised with stripes, like I'd had you up against a picket fence!''

She let go of his erection to unbutton her bell-bottoms as she demurely replied, ''Is good thing I got long legs and we have a ladder for to hang on to. For why are you not taking off your gun belt and pants at least?''

As if to answer for him, the hatchway at the top of the ladder was rattled by someone trying to open it as a voice that sounded like old Bajo called, "Are you down there, Dandolo? Monakai wishes for to know if you know we are steaming at full speed across a calm sea!"

The gal who was obviously used to being in charge dropped her bell-bottoms all the way and stepped out of them in her *zapatas* while she called back in a voice of authority, "I would not have shoved this throttle to full speed if I wished for to be becalmed with the *marina federale* searching for us under steam! Tell Monakai to steer north-northwest for that delta until I have further instructions for him. At the moment we are adjusting the machinery. Is very delicate work and we do not wish for to be disturbed!"

She laughed softly as her crew member went away. Longarm had to chuckle. But he warned her, "That old boy is sure to gossip about all this adjusting behind a bolted hatchway in the dark."

He could just make out her stark-naked form, edged in blue light, as she moved over to lean her back against the ladder and calmly ask him, *"Como coño lo quires?"*

So, seeing he'd been not only invited but urged to take her any way he wanted, Longarm just stepped up to her in his wet duds and gun rig to take her chilled firm flesh in his arms some more.

She started to protest the wet cloth and chilly belt buckle against her bare breasts and belly. Then she hugged him closer with an amused remark about novelty, and hooked one of her naked thighs over the grips of his six-gun as she pleaded, *"No me friegues!"*

So, seeing she seemed to feel he was fooling around too long, he guided the raging tip between her twitching love-lips and thrust up into the warmest place in the engine room, next to the engine.

"Dios mio! Is too big!" she gasped, even as she lifted

the other thigh to make room for all he could offer. It worked better once he'd grabbed hold of the ladder with one of her knees hooked over either elbow. She hung on to a step above their heads for leverage as she moved her hips in unconscious time with the hissing and sucking sounds of the nearby steam engine. Then they came together fast.

Longarm had been braced all the while for another knock on the door right above them. But as nobody came but them, he figured it was just possible he wasn't the first passenger Irena might have adjusted her machinery with. So he was game when she suggested they do it a tad friendlier. He hung his hat and gun on handy valve handles, and draped his wet duds over the boiler as they tried it on the duckboards with her on top. He said he didn't care if *he* wound up with a purple stripe or so up his back, and there was a lot to be said for letting a gal who'd been climbing the rigging since childhood squat over your partly satisfied privates to bring them back to full attention with a friendly game of stoop tag.

In the end they wound up dog style with the blue burner light on her firm young *nalgas* reminding Longarm of another gal he'd had this way by moonlight. It sure beat all how gals who got more exercise aboard most anything that bucked wound up with the same shapely behinds, be they blond or brunette. As he thrust in and out of Irena, he wondered idly who was doing this to the young Widow Stover this same moonlit night. For *somebody* had to be, damn his liver and lights. Old Kim had been a lot like this pretty little crook when it came to country customs, and damn it, the best ones always seemed to be the ones a man just had no business messing with.

Kim had been a rich widow out to marry up with him and settle him down, while this one seemed anxious to lead him and his badge down the primrose path to perdition. And so, in that friendly conversational tone that dog style

157

seemed to inspire, he warned her, "I'm fixing to come in you again. But please don't tell me what you were planning to do with this boat, or that Gatling gun, north of the border!"

She arched her spine to take it deeper as she sobbed a promise not to let him in on any crimes she had planned for the near future. So a fine time was had by all, and less than an hour later they got dressed and went back on deck, where Irena ordered yet another crew member to go below and keep an eye on the dials Longarm had marked with his pencil. Longarm assumed she was unaware or didn't care that the smell of sweaty screwing hung in the air in an unventilated room for a spell.

Seeing she was yelling other orders, as if to make up for lost time, Longarm moved up in the bows to get out of the way and enjoy a smoke without being rude. He only had a few of those cigars El Gato had given him, and he didn't want to have to offer.

The full moon was shining over his left shoulder, painting his shadow across the deck as he lit up facing north. So even though he was lighting a *claro,* he still spotted the *other* shadow of some sneak moving up behind him.

Longarm shook out the match and exhaled a cloud of unsuspicious smoke as the other one made his move. His aim, it seemed, had been to shove Longarm overboard. But things turned out the other way when the intended victim grabbed a stay to crab sideways, trip the murderous son of a bitch, and rabbit-punch him as he lunged with outstretched arms through the space where Longarm had been standing.

As his moonlight attacker dove headfirst over the rail with a yell, cut off by a splash nobody else seemed to notice, Longarm took another drag on the *claro* and murmured dryly, "That was strike three, Bajo."

Chapter 14

Longarm found a cubbyhole with a door he could bolt, and caught a few safe hours of sleep before a change in the motion of the vessel and bright sunlight through the one porthole woke him up. He went out on deck to see they were heeled over at full sail in such breeze as a desert shore next to a stagnant inland sea had to offer. The sky above was that shade of blue Mexicans liked to paint tables and window frames. They were coasting close inshore to take full advantage of the onshore airs. The ominous black cliffs over yonder were likely lava, cooled and sharpened by seawater.

He went aft to the cockpit to find Irena talking to the helmsman she had at the wheel that morning. That didn't surprise Longarm. What did surprise Longarm was that Bajo seemed alive and well behind the wheel.

Irena smiled up at Longarm and said, ''Come below with me and I'll have my galley crew serve you some breakfast. Have you seen Monakai anywhere this morning? Nobody seems to know where he's been sleeping, and he *is* supposed to be standing watch!''

Longarm was too thunderstruck to mutter more than, ''Well, we sure do live and learn!''

He hadn't expected that to mean anything to her. As he followed her through the hatchway forward of the cockpit, she confided in a softer tone, "I am afraid for the Islander's safety. Is not true he was allowed to treat me as you did last night, *toro mio*. But some of my *muchachos* may have thought I favored him a little. He learned for to sail aboard a Yanqui whaling ship, and perhaps some confused the way I relied on his sailing skills with a desire for his big brown *pipi*. Not that I have ever *seen* it, of course. Is difficult for to keep such secrets aboard ship, eh?"

He said he wasn't interested in Monakai's big tool, but suggested, "You could be right about somebody on board having had a jealous hard-on last night. We'd best behave ourselves until we can sneak off to a more private love nest in Yuma. How soon were you figuring on getting us to Yuma, by the way?"

She sat them both down in the small main salon, and called forward for some coffee for the both of them and a plate of Moors and Christians or beans with rice for Longarm's breakfast.

As they waited, she explained they'd be moving up through the swampy and uncharted Colorado Delta before sundown if these breezes held. She said, "Is better to approach the delta under full steam with the sails furled for not to attract attention, eh?"

He asked if it might not be even slicker to sneak in the last few miles by moonlight, adding, "The seaward reaches of that whole delta are south of the border, ain't they?"

Irena nodded and said, "With a *marina federale* base guarding the main channel. We must have some daylight for to navigate the channels we must choose instead. This big cutter draws more water than my own little schooner, and even *she* has trouble finding her way through the tule flats when the muddy waters of the Gila and Colorado meet the sea in ever-changing patterns."

He said he followed her drift, and then a Mexican kid

brought a tray back to them. The coffee was strong, and the government-issue rice was a nice change from most working-class Mexican cooking. Spanish-speaking folks liked rice almost as much as Chinese did. But it didn't grow in most of Mexico. So only El Presidénte and his own got to eat any rice worth mentioning, and Longarm's pirate pals were out to consume all the government grub on board. Longarm didn't ask Irena what she and her crew planned to do with this cutter farther along. He was afraid she'd tell him, and he'd already exceeded his instructions just a bit.

Irena left before he'd finished. Once he had, he took the empty cups and his plate forward to the galley. They didn't seem to have any chores for him, so he went on deck and seemed to mostly get in the way, until he found a place on the foredeck to display some landlubber skills.

That Gatling gun had ridden out the storm under a trap, but it was still overdue for some stripping and cleaning. Made like the first Winchesters from both steel and brass, the multibarreled death-grinder tended to corrode fast wherever sweat or salt water could set up odd little electrical currents where the two metals met.

Longarm carefully cleaned and oiled the Gatling, rubbed flecks of green corrosion off the top layer of its .45-55-405 brass, and as long as he was at it, cleaned and oiled his Big Fifty too. He did as careful a job as he knew how. It was still way the hell short of noon when he'd finished. So he smoked and stared off across the sunlit waves until Irena Dandolo joined him with more coffee and grub to allow they were making good time and ask him to tell her more about that private session he had planned for Yuma.

So they sat cross-legged to dine on sea rations by the Gatling, and he explained he figured on some paper-chasing once she got them all to Yuma. He said, "I have to paw through a whole mess of local files for homestead claims, property deeds, transfers of property, and so forth. It's high summer, and I fear the government offices in Yuma will have picked up bad habits from you Mexican folks, no offense. I ain't saying it's bad to shut down for *la siesta* when it's a hundred and change in the shade. I'm saying it's a pain in the neck when an office shuts from noon to three and then don't stay open after the usual six o'clock quitting time.''

She asked what that had to do with *el rapto supremo*. So he fought back the temptation to feel her up on deck in broad daylight as he explained, ''I don't know how long it's going to take me to find what I got to look through all those files for. I do know it's likely to be a few hours on and a heap of hours off. So there's this little hotel near the plaza, with cross ventilation north and east if you pick a top-story room with any common sense. Don't tell me what you and your pals are planning to do around Yuma. Just tell me if you'd like me to include you in my siesta plans.''

She laughed and said they'd talk about it once they got there. He didn't argue. He'd read somewhere about ship-board romances being the bee's knees until it came time to get off and you both remembered where you were headed and who you were. But it was sure a swell way to pass away the hours of an otherwise tedious journey, which likely accounted for the way spinster schoolmarms and married-up whiskey drummers wound up swearing eternal love on ships and trains so often.

But it wouldn't have been prudent to while away the afternoon in a bunk with Irena, and it was too damned hot to lock himself in below in any case. So at least a million years went by as he lazed on deck in the shade of the mainsail. Then he felt the throbbing of the engine under his rump, and some son of a bitch slapped him across the face with the late afternoon sun when they suddenly lowered all sails.

Longarm rose and ambled aft just as Irena yelled from the cockpit, and he had to grab a stay as the vessel heeled into a turn at full speed.

Back by the wheel he saw Irena staring hard to the east through a long brass spyglass. Following her gaze, he spied a smoke plume on the horizon. Irena lowered her telescope and ordered a youth in floppy white cotton to go aloft. As he pulled himself hand over hand up the ratlines, Irena nodded to Longarm and sighed, "Monakai was the best lookout we had. I told you he had learned the ropes aboard a whaling ship. But I fear he must have fallen over the side last night."

Longarm didn't want to talk about that, so he asked what else was new.

Irena pointed at the distant smoke plume and replied, "Is burning oil and not coal in a careless fashion. That is for why is so black. When we turn, *they* turn. It has to be a *federale* gunboat out of San Luis Rio Colorado. Faster than us under steam. That is for why that smoke plume keeps getting closer! Do you think we could move that Gatling gun aft, for to give them a running gunfight if they catch us out here on open water?"

Longarm glanced the way they were headed to see that the north horizon, maybe three miles off, lay string-straight and oddly greener than the ripples all around.

Figuring they had at least half an hour to go, he asked her if she knew what sort of guns she had in mind for her running gunfight. When she told him the Mexican gunboats on the lower Colorado were mostly armed with Hotchkiss one-pounders outfitted with boiler-plate shields, he had to shake his head wearily and explain how her notion added up to a total waste of hope.

He said, "That Gatling fires cheap .45-55 rifle rounds. A good marksman can barely hope to stay on the target paper with his Springfield .45-70 at four hundred yards. Let's say the Gatling can sprinkle out to thrice that range, with rapid fire and pure luck taking the place of aiming. A Hotchkiss lobbing 37-millimeter shells back at you from behind an iron shield don't add up to a gunfight. It'd be as one-sided as those Spanish bullfights you folks admire, no offense.''

She insisted, ''Sometimes the bull wins, and have you forgotten that longer-ranging buffalo gun you brought aboard when we took this cutter?''

Longarm sighed and said, ''The Big Fifty can shoot straight about as far as their infernal deck gun, albeit way slower. Did you have an iron gun turret in mind for me to shoot from? That antique just ain't a true field gun, Miss Irena. Did I bounce even seven hundred grains of solid lead off their iron shield, they'd just laugh and pay me back with a pound of exploding steel.''

He craned his neck for a better view forward as he added, ''You did say you know your way through that big swamp we seem to be headed for, didn't you?''

Before she should answer, the lookout shouted, ''I can see her down to the waterline now! Is an armored gunboat and—*Dios mio! Esos cabrones* seem to be firing on us!''

The helmsman threw them hard left rudder without waiting for orders as the shell from the distant gunboat proved the lookout had guessed right about that big white puff of smoke he'd spotted. They heard the dull crump of the deck gun, followed by the whistle and far louder splash-bang when the shell went off under their wake to spout muddy water skyward.

Irena yelled up for their lookout to watch for shoal water as well, just as he let fly with another warning and they turned sharply the other way. When the second shell landed awfully close to where they'd just been, the war veteran among them grabbed the spyglass from Irena, snapping, ''They ain't ranging that tight by guesswork!''

Peering through the telescope at deck level, Longarm could only make out the smoke plume and top third of their mast. But that was enough for him to say, ''They don't have anyone in their crow's nest! They're aiming at our mast! It's the only thing they can see at this range from their point of view!''

Irena proved herself the quick-thinking descendant of long-gone sea rovers by snapping out orders about fire axes. Longarm gazed in wonder as what looked like someone's south forty of oats or barley moved across his vista at better than six knots. Then they were surrounded by more tule reeds than open water, and Irena was shouting a warning about falling timber.

The mast they'd chopped through crashed over the side with a mighty splash of muddy foam, and swung them broadside as its far end dug into the shallow bottom. But then swift machete strokes had severed every stay and, with Longarm's help, the butt end was heaved overboard and they were on their way up a broad but twisting channel.

Hence, it took a spell to figure out what the other side was up to when another one-pound shell blasted a gout of mud and chopped-up tule from the bottom just to starboard.

Their own lookout had naturally come down before they'd chopped the mast through at deck level. Longarm took the spyglass from Irena again and aimed it at the far-off smudge of dirty oil smoke. He could see how they'd done it now. He told Irena, ''they've sent their own lookout up. He can doubtless see all of us, even though we can only make out their infernal mast.''

Irena swore in Italian as well as Spanish before she pleaded, ''Can you not reach them with your long-range buffalo rifle?''

To which Longarm could only reply, ''No. They're close to three miles away and the Big Fifty has its limits, even with full elevation!''

Then another one-pounder blasted a column of muddy water over the foredeck, and he added with a sigh, ''Like Miss Mouse said to Froggie when he came a-courting, 'This may not work but we can try,' for they sure as shooting have *our* range!''

Irena tagged along as he strode forward to where he'd left the Big Fifty by that Gatling gun. The canvas tarp over the Gatling was leopard-spotted with fresh liquid mud. Longarm tore it off the .45-55-405 deck gun and spread it on the spattered planking as he got out that trading-post pocket knife and showed Irena how to cut oiled canvas patches the size of silver dollars before he went to work on both .50 and .45 ammunition on a far corner of the tarp.

Irena cut canvas with the skill of a born sail-patching gal, but she naturally asked him what in blue blazes they were doing.

Longarm explained, "My pistol balls ain't heavy enough. But like Miss Goldilocks remarked on porridge, these 405-grain Gatling slugs might be just right. Heavier than this old .44-40 throws, but almost two hundred grains lighter than this Big Fifty, see?"

Irena replied, "No. I can see you can fit a smaller .45 bullet in the chamber meant for .50-caliber. *Pero* for how far can you hope to shoot with the gas escaping all around the most loose fit?"

Longarm used his teeth to pry a 600-grain Big Fifty slug from its brass cartridge before he explained, being careful not to let any black powder escape. "That's how you figure to help me, with all those pretty patches. Hand me one and I'll show you."

She did. He centered the canvas over the open end of the Big Fifty shell and picked up a smaller Gatling round. He bit its head off, being careful not to dent the lead too deeply with teeth that were harder by far, and seated the 405-grain slug where six hundred grains had been.

It wasn't easy. The oiled canvas didn't want to let him. He had to really push, saying, "This stout patch puckered all around this lighter bullet ought to give us result something like you got with an old-time Kentucky rifle. They used to ram a .31-caliber ball down a .36-caliber bor with a cloth or deerskin patch. It was the patch, not the ball, as sealed the gasses and gripped the spiral lands as it tore on out the muzzle. Patch and ball part company within yards of the same, of course. But by that time the spinning lead is on its way to the target. So what the hell.''

Rising to his feet, Longarm loaded the Big Fifty with his ragged-looking improvisation, moved over to the rail, and elevated by guess and by God to let fly an experimental shot.

They couldn't say whether anyone aboard that distant gunboat had noticed. So they picked up the mess they'd just made and moved aft to the cockpit, and Irena's spyglass, as he reloaded the smoking Big Fifty. Another one-pounder came down to spatter muddy water over the taffrail as they spread the tarp, patches, and cartridges in different stages of disrepair on the duckboards of the cockpit.

Bajo, cowering forward near the stub of the mast, wailed some stupid suggestion about surrender. But nobody bothered to answer. For even the galley boy knew he'd go up against the wall if the other side got hold of his skinny young ass.

Irena, peering through her spyglass, said that *chingado federale* lookout seemed alive and well as ever.

Longarm growled, ''Ain't out to kill him. I only need to rattle him enough to chase him down from his crow's nest.''

He fired again.

She said, ''I don't know where you're putting those bullets. But I can tell you they are not landing close enough to that *cabrone* for to notice!''

He fired again, and proceeded to jam another Gatling slug into the space meant for a bigger one as he decided, ''I must have the elevation wrong then. Figuring the direction is no big deal. So I'm going over or under.''

He braced the Big Fifty on his thigh and decided to try just a tad less than a full forty-five-degree elevation, since there was nothing in this world he could do if he was already dropping them short.

He pulled the trigger, going through motions he felt to be futile as he tried to come up with something better. He had no way, from a good three miles away, to even guess where his small desperate shots might be hitting. But aboard the gunboat the lookout and conning crew on the bridge could see an occasional splash or even hear a metallic clang as a born marksman's Kentucky windage paid off.

Not knowing this, Longarm suggested Irena's crew set some flaming oil-soaked rags adrift in a pot from the galley, explaining, "Whether they think they hit us somewhere else or not, the smoke drifting amid all the reed islands we're passing might make us tougher to aim at."

So they got cracking as he kept loading and shooting off almost a round a minute. Nobody could have planned it, but just as somebody has to win every lottery, a lucky shot glanced off the steel mast to pink the lookout and whine eerily on to smack their funnel with a mighty bang of flattened lead on steel. So it took a spell for the lookout to gingerly peer over the rim of his crow's nest, blood running down one cheek, to see a low pall of oily smoke drifting across the not-at-all-certain channel the outlaws had headed into.

He called down, "I think we've hit them. Fire at the same azimuth and elevation!"

The gun crew obliged as the lookout searched the bottom of his cockpit in vain for the binoculars he'd dropped somewhere. So their one-pounders landed wide, with change, as *El Tiberon Blanco* moved deeper into the tule reeds, her centerboard up, but still stirring up thick gobs of bottom silt from time to time.

The skipper of the gunboat didn't care to risk a grounding as he stood out to sea and kept lobbing shells into that big black cloud of smoke. By the time it had cleared, a deckhand had brought the lookout his dropped binoculars. One lens still worked well enough for him to shout down with some confidence, "We've sunk her! Is nothing where she was but chopped up tule and an oil slick!"

So they told him to come down and get his scalp patched up as they turned to head back to San Luis Rio Colorado and the telegraph there. El Presidénte was going to be so pleased with them for sinking El Brazo Largo and a whole pirate crew, even if it had been a government cutter and they'd had orders to watch out for that schooner Dandolo was said to be planning another smuggling run aboard.

So the sun had gone down by the time *El Tiberon Blanco* limped back to the main channel, north of the border, to make for the winking lights of Yuma on the last of its fuel oil.

Smoking the last of El Gato's cigars on the foredeck, Longarm was more surprised than alarmed when the bows swung sharply for the higher left bank of the river. As Irena ran them aground in the soft mud of the shallows, Longarm grunted, "Right. No sense or profit in explaining a Mexican cutter to the Arizona authorities when you don't have to."

He moved forward to regard the jump to the muddy bank without a whole lot of anticipation. He didn't think he could make it, and he jumped farther than most. Irena had long legs for a gal, but not *that* long. So what if he took off his boots and carried her?

Then Irena had joined him in the grounded bows just as someone on shore softly called out, *"Conozco una guapa que es no puta,"* which was sort of inane. Then, having been told the cuss on the dark bank knew a fine-looking gal who wasn't a whore, Irena assured the cuss her parrot was sick, which had to be code.

Longarm knew he'd guessed right when the jolly rogues on shore got a long plank out to them in no time. It was mighty springy, and Longarm was glad Irena had gone first when she helped him and the Big Fifty ashore by taking the rifle from him as he was commencing to lose his balance in the tricky light.

Once she had all her crew ashore, Irena ran back aboard as if she'd forgotten something. When Longarm started to follow, she told him not to. So he never did.

A few minutes later, as she rejoined him and the others massed on the bank, he followed her drift. *El Tiberon Blanco* backed off the mud flats with the last of its steam turning its screw in reverse. She didn't have to tell him the sluggish current would carry the abandoned vessel downstream to most anywhere. It was obvious she and her crew only cared to hide exactly where they might have gotten off.

He saw why a few minutes later as he followed Irena and her mixed bag of about two dozen crew members along the bank to where another vessel was tied up in a willowy bend. It was tough to make out in the dark, as they'd doubtless figured when they'd put in there, but he could see she was far smaller than the cutter they'd stolen, and he could make out her two masts against the night sky above Yuma.

He chuckled fondly and told Irena, "Don't ever invite a United States lawman aboard or offer to show him your bill of lading after you pull a stunt like this, you sneaky little thing."

She answered in an innocent schoolmarm voice, "Why Custis, what are you accusing me and mine of being up to?"

He laughed and said, "Like the love that dare not speak its name, there are business transactions along this border it's best to say no more about. I'm going on to that place in town we were talking about. You go on about your unstated business, if you've a mind to. I don't want to know a thing about it. It hurts just as much to lie to my boss as it does to peach on my pals, so . . ."

"I'm going with you," she said, turning to a follower or kinsman Longarm hadn't met before to rattle off some orders in North Italian. Then she scampered after Longarm to grab his one free elbow and demurely ask if he thought they'd let her in the hotel with him if the two of them were wearing pants.

He laughed and said they'd let him in with a sheep, as long as he was willing to pay for a double. So they ambled on along the bank until they were out of earshot of her crew and she could tell him how dirty she meant to treat him the moment she had him in bed behind another locked door.

He said he wasn't scared, and added they'd have all night before he had to mosey over to the Yuma hall of records and grope through all those musty papers.

Irena sighed and said, "I wish your business here was simple as my own. We only have to unload a modest cargo for some Yanqui fruit growers."

He warned, "Don't *tell* me about your infernal smuggling, *querida*! I already know you combined business with pleasure by luring that gunboat away from the main channel so's your own schooner could sneak on by. I'd just have to turn you in if I knew for certain what you just smuggled into these United States!"

She asked, "For why? Was Mexico's unjust *export* duties we avoided, while we did a favor for El Gato. Is no Yanqui duties on *semillas*, is there?"

To which he could only reply, "I don't know. What sort of seeds are we talking about?"

She shrugged and said, "For to grow avocodos, dates, olives, and a dry-climate orange tree. Some Yanqui settlers are most interested in new crops for these irrigated bottomlands. So they pay well for new crops to experiment with, if only El Presidénte would let us keep most of the money and . . . For why are you hugging me, Custis? Can't you wait?"

He said, "I can and I will and I mean to screw you silly, because I suspect you just saved me a whole heap of paperwork, you sweet-smuggling little thing!"

Chapter 15

It took two days, and Irena said she was glad. Longarm never did find anything out about Trader Wolfram and Rosalinda's other sister. But once he'd settled on the desert claim of a late Doctor Dundee, he got out there just as the hot dry siesta time was commencing, lest he miss one member of the gang he'd run to ground at last.

So Harmony Drake, Centerfire Max, and Goldmine Gloria were enjoying a noonday repast served by Spud Travis, the junior member of the bunch, as Longarm let fly with the Big Fifty outside.

The thunderous report gained the undivided attention of all four crooks, an hour's ride up the Gila Trail from Yuma, just as Longarm had intended.

He had his peepsight trained on a gun loop cut through the thick 'dobe wall beside the stout oaken door of the low-slung ranch house as he heard someone shouting, "Who fired that cannon and where are you at?"

Longarm knew that to those in the house he could be most anywhere along a ragged cactus hedge between their dusty dooryard and the dead and dried-out citrus grove behind him. He let them guess just where as he called back not unkindly, "Who've you been expecting, your fairy godmother? I'd be the same U.S. Deputy Marshal Custis Long you left for dead on that ant pile over by Growler Wash. So now you are all under arrest, and I don't really care whether you want to come quietly or not. You've surely neglected the trees and shrubbery around your late husband's homestead, Miss Gloria. Didn't anyone ever tell you irrigation ditches don't work unless you pump water into 'em now and again?''

Inside the house a sweaty-faced Harmony Drake shot a thunderstruck look at his doxie and snarled, ''You dumb cunt! I might have known you had to brag! You were only supposed to be buttering him up aboard that train!''

Goldmine Gloria, sweating in her own right, brushed a strand of limp blond hair from her flushed forehead as she protested, ''I never did! Nobody in town could have told him either. Are we going to fuss about how he found us or are we going to *do* something about it?''

Drake turned to the outlaw peering through the gun slit to ask, ''Can you make any of 'em out, Centerfire?''

Centerfire Max, so called for the single-cinched Mexican saddle he'd once ridden up Montana way rather than for the serious rifle rounds in his Winchester Yellowboy, eased the barrel of the weapon further out the gun slot as he tersely replied, ''Sun's in my damned eyes. He likely knew it *would* be when he chose this hour to come calling, the tricky son of a bitch!''

Across the way, Longarm shouted, ''The warrant I have on you says dead or alive, and you've never done nothing to endear yourself to me, Harmony. If you ain't coming out, I reckon we'll have to come in. For it's really starting to get hot out here.''

He waited a polite count of a hundred times Mississippi while, in the house, Harmony snarled, ''Don't nobody fall for that. He never up and said any of you others ain't as wanted as this child. He's trying that divide-and-conquer shit!''

From over near the fireplace, where he'd hunkered to douse the cooking coals, the kid called Spud looked up to ask just what Harmony meant. So Goldmine Gloria said, "Nothing. Stuff a sock in it, Harmony. He's doing all right without your help."

At the slot, Centerfire groused, "I told you all the other night we should have killed the big bastard! It ain't as if he didn't have a rep for tracking! But no, we had to slicker the best tracker they got by playing Here We Go 'round the Mulberry Bush across the damned old desert with him."

Then Longarm had finished counting and let fly with the Big Fifty. Guessing which opening they might be staring out from, and knowing a right-handed gunslick would be peeking out with his right eye, from the lower corner to Longarm's right, he aimed at the angle formed by sill and jam, to send a fistful of splinters, a bowlful of blood and bone, and all of Centerfire Max flying back from the gun loop as his dead trigger finger fired an even more frightening shot inside the confines of the little 'dobe!

"Oh, Jesus!" wailed Spud Travis as, spattered with gobs of blood and brain matter, he leaped to his feet and tore out the back way as fast as he could run.

He got halfway to the corral before he noticed someone had been at those ponies that should have been under the shady *toldo* above the watering trough. Then he made an even worse mistake and lit out afoot across the flat, moving pretty good despite the heat and his high heels and spurs. Longarm didn't spot him before he'd made it almost two full furlongs from one corner of the house. Then Longarm called out to him, saw that only seemed to speed the kid up, and fired.

He'd already ducked and rolled by the time his heavy buffalo round cartwheeled the running Spud Travis into a clump of pear, from which he would never rise under his own power. So when Harmony Drake blazed away at the Big Fifty's smoke through another window, glass and all,

Longarm was grinning through another gap in the hedge entirely. He knew nobody with a lick of sense would still be standing behind all that gunsmoke drifting through the shattered window. So he held his own fire for now.

Inside the house, Goldmine Gloria was saying, "He's as crazy as I heard! He's got no other lawmen with him! He aims to take you in alone! Whatever makes the man act so contrary?"

Harmony almost snarled, "What makes womankind ask such totally stupid questions? Can't you see he wants to take me alone because he refused help the other night and bragged he could handle me without any? Centerfire was right. We should have killed him when we had the chance. I was a fool to let you talk us into doubling back on our own trail like we done. When a body gets away from a lawman like Longarm, he's got no business playing kid games!"

The brassy blond widow woman who owned the dusted-out farm said, "We'd have never been found out if you hadn't had to go into Yuma and get caught that time. I told you everyone had me down as the rightful owner of this property, under my married name, not as the Goldmine Gloria of dubious fame along the Owlhoot Trail. I told you boys to let me run grub and snake-medicine out here whilst the law lost interest in us all, but—"

"You're fixing to make a deal with him, ain't you," her paramour and partner in crime demanded.

The brassy blonde sighed wearily and moaned, "Oh, Lord, hang some crepe on your nose. Your brain just died. I'd have turned you in for the bounty weeks ago if that had been my plan when I took you under my wing. How many times do I have to tell you the big job I have planned for up Tombstone way will pay more than I could get for you, Frank, Jesse, and the Kid? I don't need any damned bounty money, honey. I need some tough hairpins to back my play when I clean out that bullion shipment next month!"

Harmony moved to another window, six-gun in hand, as he grumbled a lot about recent developments. She said soothingly, "I know we seem to have been too tricky with Longarm for our own good, honey. I'm sorry I got all the boys killed. But we had to keep this homespread to work out of. We *still* need a place to hole up with that freight wagon of bullion we've been planning on. There's just no way you could freight tons of silver out before they cooled off, and once we get rid of that one pest outside, and recruit a few more gunslicks—"

Then she screamed as Longarm, having caught a glimpse of her nervous pacing when she passed a wall mirror, let fly a buffalo round that shattered both another window pane and the wall mirror, to inspire a dive for the floor and considerable wetness between her already sweat-soaked thighs.

Harmony blazed back at the smoke curling up from the cactus across the way, then ducked and rolled for the other shattered window before Longarm could return his fire.

Crouched below the level of the other sill, reloading, Harmony muttered, "He's still using that slow but sure buffalo rifle. He must have picked up another six-gun by now. He must be out to rattle us by busting things up with them big slugs."

Goldmine Gloria moved toward the slot by the door with the Yellow Boy that Centerfire wasn't using any more as she licked her lips and said, "It seems to be working. He's got me scared skinny and *you* seem to be the one he's after!"

Harmony Drake's voice chilled ten degrees as he quietly asked her just how he was supposed to take that last remark.

Goldmine Gloria probably saved her blond head as she turned from the slot instead of shoving the gun muzzle out of it. She saw the sweaty but pale-faced Harmony was staring at her, rather than out the window, and she smiled wanly and said, "Honey, you're letting him get to you! Our only chance calls for our sticking together! Be a good boy and shoot the bad man for Mommy and Mommy will give you a nice blow job. He's whittled us down to where it's only two to one. But that's still two to one, if we don't lose our heads!''

It wasn't going to work. Goldmine Gloria was good at her chosen criminal career because she could almost read the mind of a mark from his or her words and expressions. Like all good confidence artists or poker players, Goldmine Gloria knew it was when words and expressions didn't quite match up that things were about to go to hell in a hack. So as her partner in bed and crime smiled boyishly and softly allowed he'd yet to see her lose her *own* head, Goldmine Gloria fired from the hip and spun Harmony away from the other window with a round of .44-40 lead in his chest.

She watched numbly as her fellow plotter and paramour twitched his last on the dusty floor amid shards of busted glass and some spatters from the more thoroughly shot Centerfire. Then she rose to move over to that wall mirror while, outside, Longarm called out, ''It's commencing to get awfully hot out here.''

The sole survivor didn't answer. She knew how much time she had. She knew Longarm was alone out there and had no way of seeing in. So that gave her time to strip off her sweated-up and pissed-in shift, rub a damp rag over her flushed skin, and run a comb through her limp hair before she moved over to the front door, opened it a crack, and tossed the Yellow Boy out before calling, ''It's over. You won. Come on in and have some sangria I just made.''

Longarm called back, ''I have a better notion, Miss Gloria. I want you to step out on the veranda with your hands polite. Then I want the others to follow suit before we talk about any cooling drinks this here sunny afternoon.''

Goldmine Gloria stepped outside, in nothing but her high-button shoes. Longarm knew they were miles from the nearest neighbor, but it still surprised him some to see a stark naked gal with a figure like that by broad day.

Staying put in the ruined orchard behind its cactus hedge, Longarm ordered her to move clear of the gaping doorway behind her. Goldmine Gloria moved mighty interestingly as she sauntered to one side, calling across to him, "You got all three of them, Custis. There's nobody left but little old me, and I hope you understand they made me do it that night aboard the train."

Longarm sighed and shouted, "I saw how they had you covered. I have you covered better. So what say you come on across to me and all our ponies now."

She demurred girlishly. "Without any clothes on, Custis?"

He thought, then decided, "Go back inside. Put on some duds. Then I want you to do me a little favor before you come back out."

She asked what that might be. When he told her, she said he was a big meany. But just the same, she piled all the furniture together and poured lamp oil over it before she struck a match, tossed it on the pile, and came out once more, just ahead of a whole lot of smoke.

As she joined Longarm in the meager shade of the dried-out trees behind the hedge, Goldmine Gloria archly asked if he was satisfied at last, smoothing her thin gingham shift in a manner to suggest she stood ready and able to satisfy most any other commands he meant to issue.

He stared soberly across the way at the 'dobe. The smoke now issuing from all doors and windows would have been tough as all get-out to breathe, had anyone been trying. Then he nodded and said, "You must have been telling the truth. It happens, I've been told. We'll let the smoke clear. Then I'll see about loading the three of them aboard the ponies I led over this way earlier and getting all four of you to town."

Goldmine Gloria shyly said, "I have a teeny-weeny question to ask. You promise you won't fuss at me?"

He smiled thinly and replied, "I ain't mad. You shooting the last of them makes for a neater report on my part. My boss can be such an old fuss when he sends me after a want and I wind up having to kill the cuss. If you're asking whether you'll be entitled to the bounty money on old Harmony, you'll have to take that up with the powers that be. I'm a lawman, not a lawyer, and it beats me whether a gang member is entitled to claim the reward on another or not. Worth a try, I reckon. Lord knows you may need the money for your golden years by the time you get out."

Goldmine Gloria blanched and gasped, "Surely you jest! I did it for us, not the reward money! He was about to crack up and kill both of us, honey!"

Longarm nodded at the half-dozen ponies tethered back from the hedge in the meager shade of the dried-out orchard, and took one of her arms to steer her that way as he said, "Don't be so formal. Call me Deputy Long. I ain't taking you in on any federal charge. I have better things to do, and it ain't as if you met up with me the other night as pure as the driven snow. What makes you so mean, Goldmine Gloria?"

She tried in vain to pull free as she protested, "You can't turn me over to the Pinkertons. They've made up all sorts of awful lies about a poor orphan girl who was only trying to get by. I'd do anything, anything you could possibly desire of a woman, if only you'd try to see things my way!"

Longarm chuckled softly and replied, "I know you would. But I ain't sure I could think the way you do. Thanks to you, most of my regular stuff went on to Deming without me. So I had to borrow this pony and such from the Yuma law."

She gasped again in horror as he calmly produced a set of handcuffs and had her fastened to a small dead tree before she knew it.

He said, "Wait here whilst I gather up your playmates

and get us all set to ride back to town. What sort of fruit did your late husband have in mind before you let this spread go back to pure desert?''

She sobbed, ''How should I know? He said it would take seven long years before they'd bear fruit, and time's cruel teeth give a woman so few years to spare! I wanted to enjoy my youth and beauty while I had them. I *still* want those few short years, Custis! You know I've never been really wicked. Let me help you catch crooks! I know a lot of crooks I'll bet you're looking for and we'd make a great team. I can help you track crooks by day and make your nights sheer paradise because I've read this Hindu love book and memorized every page!''

Longarm began to untether three of the ponies as he wistfully remarked, ''This pretty widow lady I know up Denver way has a copy of that *Kama Sutra* some mighty imaginative Hindu wrote. Some of the positions are uncomfortable, and we found more than one just plain impossible. I'll be back directly and we can see to your comfort in the Yuma jail.''

As he started to turn away, the brassy blonde demanded in a colder tone, ''Wait. Won't you at least tell me how you found out I owned this remote homestead in the middle of nowhere?''

Longarm smiled thinly and shook his head, saying, ''Not hardly. I paid for my education and you're already too smart by half. But I can give you a hint. A smart-ass little birdy told me.''

She nodded wearily and said, ''We were afraid you might have gotten something out of Sam Ferris when the two of you were locked up together down in Puerto Peñasco.''

Then Longarm spoiled it for her by soberly shaking his head. ''If it's any comfort to you, I tried in vain to get old Sam to talk. He seemed to be sore at me for some reason.

He wasn't the one who as much as told me all about this spread outside of Yuma."

She frowned and decided, "You're conning me. You never got a chance to question any of the others. I was the only one you ever had more than a few words with, and I know *I* never told you anything!"

He leaned the empty Big Fifty against another tree and gathered up the reins as he told her, "Look on the bright side. It'll give you a puzzle to ponder late at night as you while away your jail time."

So he never told her, no matter how she cussed and pleaded all the way back to Yuma, where they parted unfriendly.

But once he got back to his home office and filed his report, his immediate superior, the crusty U.S. Marshal William Vail of the Denver District Court, seemed less than satisfied as to some details.

Thus it came to pass that on a payday afternoon, as Longarm was anxious to go calling with a bunch of violets and a copy of the *Kama Sutra* in a plain brown wrapper, he found himself literally on the carpet in Billy Vail's oak-paneled and smoke-filled back office.

A million years went by as Longarm sat smoking milder tobacco in the leather chair across a cluttered desk from the older, shorter, and far beefier Billy Vail, who seemed to enjoy reading reports over and over as the banjo clock on the wall ticked away whole minutes of fun a man could be having most anywhere else.

At last the older lawman lowered the typed-up first copy with a puzzled sigh and declared, "All right. You did well enough, I reckon. I sent you to bring back Harmony Drake and you at least produced that sepia-toned photograph they took before they nailed the coffin lid in Yuma. You paid for that out of your own pocket, of course?"

Longarm nodded soberly and said, "I owned up to his death in that report. I confess off the record I got a deal on the burials. Knowing how you feel about us putting in for bounty money, I suggested a pal on the Yuma force might as well, provided he'd care to take those dead boys off my hands, along with Goldmine Gloria.''

Vail nodded his bullet head curtly and said, ''I ain't puzzled about the way Harmony Drake and so many of his pals wound up dead, and you did good by turning that confidence gal over to the Pinks and saving the taxpayers the needless expenses of a federal trial.''

He chewed thoughtfully on his evil-smelling but expensive cigar and decided, ''I'm taking your word you were in hot pursuit and never noticed you were in Mexico until you had that little misunderstanding with the greaser law, albeit sometimes these reports of yours push reasonable to highly unlikely. What I'm still trying to fathom is who put you on to that half-abandoned desert homestead owned by Goldmine Gloria Weaver under the name of the Widow Dundee.''

He brandished Longarm's typed-up report like a sword as he added, ''Sure, it all works after the fact. You say that once you got back to Yuma, figuring the gang had needed a good reason to double back there after such a wide circle through Old Mexico, you spent a few hours at the Yuma hall of records, narrowed it down to half-a-dozen possibles, and just rode about on a borrowed horse and saddle until you came to the right one.''

Longarm nodded. ''It was all those dead fruit trees that gave the show away, Boss. Over an acre of expensive citrus saplings boxed in by a carefully transplanted cactus hedge. I saw right off how someone had put a heap of thought and hope into what had once been a tidy little experimental farm. That's what you call it when you try to grow irrigated stuff that's never growed on a desert before: an experimental farm.''

Vail growled, ''You said it was an experimental farm homesteaded by a retired doctor and his somewhat younger wife in this report. I asked how come you *knew* where to *look,* damn it!''

Longarm nodded and said, ''I reckon I got ahead of my story. It all begins on a train, where a confidence woman who's really out to free a lover from a poor innocent lawman conned him good by pretending to be a trained nursing sister.''

Vail nodded and said, ''I heard about you and that nursing sister on the Pine Ridge Reservation. I can see how she'd have to put on a better than average act with a cuss so interested in medical matters.''

Longarm smiled sheepishly and confessed, ''Goldmine Gloria sold me with some technical jargon you'd seldom read in the *Police Gazette*. So once I figured she'd only been conning me, I still knew she had to know more about medicine than your average outlaw's doxie.''

Vail nodded grudgingly and said, ''I follow your drift. But ain't it a long reach from a gal who might have read some medical books to the widow of a doc who'd left her a homestead out in the desert?''

Longarm shook his head and said, ''Not hardly. She lured me off the train in another part of that desert with a lie about the trader there being a retired doc growing oranges and such under irrigation. A half truth makes a mighty good lie, and I've noticed a heap of crooks use the same when pressed for convincing bullshit. But it only came to me when a Mex pal told me how lots of Anglo settlers had been experimenting in the desert around Yuma with exotic crops that the lying gal might have fed me a half truth about another retired doc entirely. Once *that* came to me, it was easy enough to scout through the local files and cut their trail. How many doctors marry young wives and file homestead claims in a given neighborhood, for Pete's sake? I never meant to hold out on you when I wrote that report up on the train, still feeling sort of coy. I reckon was still enjoying my little joke on her. I hope she loses heaps of sleep in the years to come trying to figure out how any gal as smart as her slipped up with somebody dumb as me. Can I go now? I promised a lady supper at Romero's come payday night.''

Vail laughed despite himself and said, "Go on. But just one thing more, Custis. This report says you wound up in Yuma last Thursday. So how do you account for not leaving town for another three days?"

To which Longarm could only reply, "Goldmine Gloria reminded me of a book that Mex pal I told you about had never read. So I bought a copy. And then, of course, I had to translate it some."

Watch for

LONGARM AND THE COUNTERFEIT CORPSE

212th in the bold LONGARM series
from Jove

Coming in August!

If you enjoyed this book, subscribe now and get...

TWO FREE

A $7.00 VALUE—

If you would like to read more of the very best, most exciting, adventurous, action-packed Westerns being published today, you'll want to subscribe to True Value's Western Home Subscription Service.

Each month the editors of True Value will select the 6 very best Westerns from America's leading publishers for special readers like you. You'll be able to preview these new titles as soon as they are published, *FREE* for ten days with no obligation!

TWO FREE BOOKS

When you subscribe, we'll send you your first month's shipment of the newest and best 6 Westerns for you to preview. With your first shipment, two of these books will be yours as our introductory gift to you absolutely *FREE* (a $7.00 value), regardless of what you decide to do. If

you like them, as much as we think you will, keep all six books but pay for just 4 at the low subscriber rate of just $2.75 each. If you decide to return them, keep 2 of the titles as our gift. No obligation.

Special Subscriber Savings

When you become a True Value subscriber you'll save money several ways. First, all regular monthly selections will be billed at the low subscriber price of just $2.75 each. That's at least a savings of $4.50 each month below the publishers price. Second, there is never any shipping, handling or other hidden charges—*Free home delivery*. What's more there is no minimum number of books you must buy, you may return any selection for full credit and you can cancel your subscription at any time. A TRUE VALUE!

LONGARM

Explore the exciting Old West with
one of the men who made it wild!